Candy was originally published in 1958 by the Olympia Press in Paris under the pseudonym Maxwell Kenton, but its true authors were Terry Southern and Mason Hoffenberg. Although Olympia publisher Maurice Girodias knew the book was of exceptional quality and encouraged the authors to use their real names, Southern, who was trying to sell a children's book to a publisher, refused. So in the 1958 Olympia catalog, there appeared this notice, written by Southern: "Maxwell Kenton is the pen name of an American nuclear physicist, formerly prominent in atomic research and development who, in February 1957, resigned his post 'because I found the work becoming more and more philosophically untenable,' and has since devoted himself fully to creative writing."

Girodias says he bought the rights to *Candy* after Southern sent him the following outline: "A sensitive, progressive-school humanist . . . comes from Wisconsin to New York's Lower East Side to be an art student, social worker, etc., and to find (unlike her father) 'beauty in mean places.'"And that's exactly what happens in this delightful novel. A takeoff on *Candide, Candy* satirizes American culture through the adventures of its protagonist, who has a "heart too big to deprive men." Candy is taken advantage of by an assortment of eccentrics, including her father's twin brother (in her unconscious father's hospital room); a Mexican gardener; an aging telegram messenger; Dr. Krankeit, a psychiatrist and the author of *Masturbation Now!*; a thieving hunchback; and a gynecologist who performs an exam on Candy in full view of gaping diners at a Greenwich Village café.

TERRY SOUTHERN was born in 1924 in Texas, the son of a pharmacist. He attended Southern Methodist University, then entered the Army in 1943. After the war, he enrolled at the University of Chicago and later Northwestern ("because it was a much groovier scene") before moving to Paris. His first novel, *Flesh and Filigree,* was published in 1958 in England and later appeared in the United States. Southern's other works include the novels *The Magic Christian* (1960), *Blue Movie* (1970), and *Texas Summer* (1992); as well as the story and essay collection *Red-Dirt Marijuana and Other Tastes* (1967). He is also known for his screenplay collaborations: *Easy Rider* with Dennis Hopper and Peter Fonda, *Dr. Strangelove* with Stanley Kubrick, and *Barbarella.* Terry Southern died in New York City in 1995.

MASON HOFFENBERG, an American poet, was one of Olympia Press's assembly line of writers. Two of his more popular Olympia works were *A Sin for Breakfast* and *Until She Screams.* Hoffenberg met Terry Southern in Paris in the late 1940s, and their collaboration came about after Southern got stuck on *Candy* and asked Hoffenberg to help him finish. Mason Hoffenberg died in New York in 1986, at the age of 64.

Candy

Candy

Terry Southern and
Mason Hoffenberg

GROVE
PRESS

The edition was specially created in 1994 for Book-of-the-Month Club by arrangement with Sterling Lord Literistic, Inc. This edition copyright © 1994 by Book-of-the-Month Club.

Published simultaneously in Canada
Printed in the United States of America

Library of Congress Cataloging-in-Publication Data

Southern, Terry.
    Candy / Terry Southern and Mason Hoffenberg.
        p.   cm.
    ISBN 0-8021-3429-7
    1. Young women—Sexual behavior—Fiction.   I. Hoffenberg, Mason.
II. Title.
PS3569.O8C3   1996
813'.54—dc20   95-49490

Grove Press
841 Broadway
New York, NY 10003

02   10 9 8 7 6

To
Hadj and Zoon

one

1

"I've read *many* books," said Professor Mephesto, with an odd finality, wearily flattening his hands on the podium, addressing the seventy-six sophomores who sat in easy reverence, immortalizing his every phrase with their pads and pens, and now, as always, giving him the confidence to slowly, artfully dramatize his words, to pause, shrug, frown, gaze abstractly at the ceiling, allow a wan wistful smile to play at his lips, and repeat quietly, *"many* books . . ." A grave nod of his magnificent head, and he continued: "Yes, and in my time I've traveled widely. They say travel broadens one—and I've . . . no doubt that it does." Here he pretended to drop some of his lecture notes and, in retrieving them, showed his backside to the class, which laughed appreciatively. Professor Mephesto's course, *Contemporary Ethics,* was one of the most popular in the school. In addition to being so highly intellectual and abstract, the professor was a regular guy, not just a simple

11

armchair crackpot. "Yes, I've no doubt that it does," he said softly, keeping a straight face as he adjusted his notes, and now letting a slight edge enter his voice—because, having given them the laugh at that point, he was now setting them up for the high seriousness to follow—this being his formula: one part tomfoolery, two parts high seriousness. "And in my travels, I've seen . . . *beauty* in every form. I've seen the rainbow on Mont Blanc, and I've seen the illuminated manuscripts of the Flemish monks where every page took seven monks two years to produce! God, they're lovely! Yes, I've strolled through the dew-sparkling Gardens of Babylon in the dawn of a summer morning, and I've seen the birds of paradise stand at eventide against the white glittering marble of the Taj Mahal. God, what a *sight!*" He paused to touch his temple, as though nearly overwhelmed. "Yes, I've seen the . . . *wonders of the world* . . .I've seen the *beauty* . . . of the world . . . the Pyramids in the thunderous blood-colored dawn, and the Tower of Pisa, and the paintings of the Great Masters . . . I've seen them all. I have seen *beauty* . . . in every form. I've stood on the ancient bridge in a snow-falling morn and heard the winter peal of the silver bells, from the high towers, over the dark stone and mysterious waters of old Heidelberg. And I've seen the Great Northern Lights . . . and the *flowers of the field!*" And he leaned toward them, touching one hand, as though absently, to his hair, and he spoke with a soft, terse defiance, so that *everyone* knew how very serious he was now, ". . . and I've seen the SUN! The glorious, glorious *sun! Beauty,* I say to you, *in every form.* BUT . . . *but . . .* I'll tell you *this*": and his lip curled in a strange, almost angry way, and a tremor came into his voice, while in the lecture hall, not even a breath was heard, "I have never seen *anything* . . . to *compare* . . . with the *beauty* . . . of the . . . *human face!*"

The bell sounded at precisely that instant, for it was another curious feature of Professor Mephesto's lectures that they reached a dramatic high point at the exact second of the bell.

In the fifth row center, Candy Christian slowly closed her notebook and dropped her pen into her purse. She was sitting on the edge of her chair, holding her breath; then she gave a soft sigh and sat back limply. She felt utterly exhausted, yet exhilarated too. A great man, she thought, a truly great man. I'm in the presence of a truly great man.

She gathered up her things and filed out slowly with the others. At the door she had a glimpse of Professor Mephesto walking down the hall toward his office, clasping his notes up to his chest, talking amiably to one of the students, his arm around the boy's shoulder—a very young boy with wild hair and a sullen face. She wondered what they were saying. She wondered what *she* would say. How she would love to be a part of the conversation! Yet, what could she say? She decided to go straight to the library and read for the rest of the afternoon, then she remembered that she had promised her father she would come directly home after class and go with him to Aunt Ida's. "Darn Daddy anyway!" she said to herself.

Candy was born on Valentine's Day. Perhaps this was why she was so beautiful—or so her father often remarked, at least in the presence of others; when they were alone, however, he was inclined to be a bit strict with her—not strict so much as insensitive to her needs, or possessively solicitous. But he was, after all, only a simpleminded businessman. At any rate though, there *was* something like a Valentine about Candy—one of the expensive ones, all frills and lace, and fragrance of lavender. But she was sometimes petulant, and perhaps it was this, her *petulance*, more than her virginity, which was her flaw and her undoing.

Mr. Christian was waiting in his armchair when Candy arrived. "Hi!" he said, glancing at his watch and only half lowering the paper. "Learn anything today?" She came over and gave him a perfunctory kiss. She wanted so much to tell him about Professor Mephesto and the human face, but of course he could never understand, not in a billion billion years. "Yes, I think so," she said quietly.

"Anything wrong?" asked Mr. Christian. He didn't like to see her face in repose, or perhaps thoughtful.

"No," she sighed and gave him a tired smile as she put down her books, "just that things are a little hectic with exams coming on."

"Hmm," said her father, getting up, brushing some tobacco from his lap, looking at his watch again. "Well, we'd better get started, if we're going," he said. "I don't want to be tied up there all afternoon. I'll get the car out."

Candy went into the bathroom and quickly brushed her hair and freshened her makeup. It did so please her father for her to look nice at Aunt Ida's. Still holding the brush she stood gazing at herself in the glass. "And I've seen the glorious *sun*," she said softly, ". . . but I've never seen beauty to compare—"

Two short sharp burps from the horn of her father's new Plymouth made her start slightly and put down the brush. She turned out the bathroom light. *"Darn* Daddy anyway!" she said to herself as she hurried for the car.

two

2

Professor Mephesto was a pacifist, and today's lecture had been about War. Since he did not have a regular question-and-answer period in his lectures, he very often posed knotty problems to himself and then proceeded to answer them, as he was doing today in his closing remarks.

"I spent last summer in Stillwater, Maine, with a friend of mine, Tab Hutchins . . . it's a place of incredible beauty, Stillwater, you'll want to go there sometime. Well, Tab isn't by *our* pompous standards, an 'educated' man . . . I mean he doesn't have the robe and the scrolls, and he doesn't speak in polysyllables, but I can tell you *this:* Tab Hutchins has one of the finest minds of our time. An auto mechanic by trade, a positivist-humanist by choice, and a scholar of the classics by inclination. I always get a little thrill somehow to see old Tab crawling under one of the dilapidated trucks that the farmers around Stillwater bring for him to fix—crawling under, a volume of Plato sticking out of one pocket, a volume of Aristotle out of the other.

"Well, one day Tab and I were talking and he said to me, in that serious way of his: 'Meph, you say you're against War. You say that War never accomplished anything.'

"I said, 'That's what I say, Tab.'

"He drew on his old briar, thoughtful for a moment, and then he said:

" 'Will you answer me one question, Meph?'

" 'I'll answer it if I can, Tab,' I said.

"Tab said, 'Then what about the *American Revolution?* Do you mean to say *that* didn't accomplish anything?'

"I said, 'Do you know who it was we fought that war against, Tab?'

" 'Of course, I do,' he said, 'the British.'

"Well, I didn't say anything more for a while, and I think Tab felt that he had me all right, the way he was watching me out of the corner of his eye, and drawing on his old briar. I was looking at the truck he had been working on all morning.

" 'How's that truck running now, Tab?' I asked him.

" 'She's running fine now, Meph,' he said, 'had to tear down the differential a little, and clean a few cogs: and now she's running fine—but I *don't* believe that answers my question.'

" 'I'll answer your question, Tab,' I said, 'but let's take a drive first. I think we ought to give that truck a pragmatic test before returning it to its owner. I'll drive,' I said.

"Well, we got in and pretty soon I had the feel of the

old bus, and we were going along at a great rate, down country roads, and across, and back, along the highway for a while. It's beautiful countryside around there, and I remarked on it to Tab.

"He said, 'Yes, it is.'

"I said, 'Do you know where we are, Tab?'

"He said, 'Sure I do.'

"I said, 'All right,' and we drove on for a while, and pretty soon I asked him again, 'How do things look out there now, Tab?'

" 'Pretty much the same as they did when you asked before,' he said.

"I said, 'Do you know where we are?'

"Tab said, 'Of course, I do.'

"I said, 'Where are we, Tab?'

"He said, 'Do you want a technical answer?'

"I said, 'Yes, I do.'

"He said, 'We're on the planet World, of Solar System number one, Western Hemisphere, North American Continent, U.S.A., and I should say about seven miles northeast of Stillwater, Maine.'

"I said, 'You're wrong, Tab. We're not in the U.S.A. now; we crossed the border into *Canada* about ten minutes ago. Canada is still a British protectorate, Tab, and it's exactly what we *didn't* accomplish by the American Revolution—and yet *you* can't tell the difference! I guess that answers your question, doesn't it, Tab?' "

Clang went the bell as, with the last word, Professor Mephesto gathered up his papers and started for the door.

In the fifth row center, Candy had just written, "What about the American Revolution?" and was drawing a very heavy line under "about," when she looked up to see the young boy she had seen with the professor yesterday, coming down the aisle, unmistakably toward her.

"Are you Candy Christian?" he asked when he reached her.

"Yes."

"Meph wants to see you," he said, with a disgruntled expression, "in his office."

"What—Professor Mephesto?"

"Yes," said the boy almost with a sneer, *"Professor Mephesto."* Then he turned abruptly to leave.

"What on earth—" Candy began, but the boy stalked away.

She gathered her things and left in a hurry—and, at the doorway, she looked up and down the hall, trying to catch sight of him again, but he was not to be seen.

"Good Grief," said Candy, and walked rapidly to the girl's lounge, where she put down her books and got out her comb and makeup. "What on earth—" she kept saying, combing her hair briskly, and finally spending an unusual amount of time putting on lipstick. She was very cross now about not having gone to the library yesterday. *"Darn Daddy!"* she said, and she decided to put on a bit of eyeshadow to make her look older, more mature. Since she hadn't been able to read, or learn anything yesterday, she reasoned, the least she could do would be to *try* to look a little more intelligent. So she decided to darken her lashes a bit too—just for balance—pinched some more color into her cheeks, and tucked her blouse in tightly. Thank goodness for that at least, that she was wearing one of her smartest blouses, fresh and sweet, with her most lavishly

embroidered slip peeking over the top through the V-neck, or V-breast, one might say, it being rather low.

At last she was ready and left the lounge, and walked primly down the hall to the professor's office. At the door, she knocked very lightly, and heard almost at once the voice which she so admired.

"Come in, come in," it said grandly.

Candy pushed open the door slowly, as though she thought there might be so many books in the room it would be partially blocked.

"Come in, my dear, come in," said Professor Mephesto, standing and ushering her in with a flourish. "I was just having my afternoon drop of sherry. I hope you'll join me."

He looked at her, expectantly, his great round, somewhat red, face overflowing with the joy of his full, rich life.

"Well, I—" Candy began, but the professor was already pouring her out a small glass.

"Yes, I always have some sherry and a bit of cheese about this time of day. Some people prefer tea, but I find it lacking—a habit, I suppose, acquired during my student days at Heidelberg, and at Oxford, no doubt—still I *do* find a good sherry has body *and* edge, while tea is such a messy affair at best, don't you agree?"

"Well—" said Candy, taking the chair indicated by the professor. The girl was quite flushed for the moment—she had never had sherry in the afternoon, though she had read of such practices in the fashionable novels and knew it to be quite proper. Also, she had heard, of course, of certain students being occasionally invited to Professor

Mephesto's office and "having a drop," as it was expressed; naturally, it was mostly confined to senior and graduate students, and, even among them, it was considered a signal honor to have done so.

"This sherry was sent to me by Lucci Locco, the Portuguese humanist-symbolist poet—now living in Paris, of course—I *think* you'll find it rather good."

He took a swig himself, then encouraged the girl to do so, by raising his glass.

"*A la tienne*," he said, "to the soul of our childhood and its sinful joys—lost forever, alas! To *youth* then! And to *beauty!*"

He allowed the last of the toast to linger on his tongue, and he gave Candy a piercing look. The girl flushed terribly and sipped in obedience.

"It's about your thesis, my dear," said Professor Mephesto, turning to his paper-strewn desk, and drawing off one of those on top, "the one on 'Contemporary Human Love,' " and he leafed through two or three pages to a place where the margin was marked with a large red X.

'Good Grief,' said Candy to herself, preparing for the worst, and she started to blurt out some foolish defense in advance, but Professor Mephesto quickly went on, clearing his throat, and shaking the papers once or twice:

"Here we are. Now here, you say: 'To give of oneself—fully—is not merely a duty prescribed by an outmoded superstition, it is a beautiful and thrilling privilege.' "

He put down the paper and looked at the girl expectantly, raising his glass of sherry again.

"Just what did you mean there, my dear?"

Candy squirmed a bit in her chair.

"But—but," she stammered, "isn't it right? Isn't that what *you* said? I was almost sure that—"

Professor Mephesto rose from his seat, clasping his hands together and looking at the ceiling.

"Isn't it *right?*" he marveled. "Oh my dear! My dear precious girl—of course, it's *right!* So very right!"

He paced about the office, intoning:

" 'To give of oneself—*fully*—is not merely a duty prescribed by an outmoded superstition, it is a beautiful and *thrilling* privilege!' "

He sat down again, and put a hand out to the girl, as though in an effort to express some extremely abstract feeling, but then finding it ineffable, let it drop, as though it were useless to try, onto her knee.

"And the burdens—the needs of man," he said with soft directness to her, "are so *deep* and so—*aching.*"

Candy involuntarily shuddered just slightly and looked down at the big fat hand on her leg—though, of course, she did not see it as that, but as the great, expressive hand of the Master—the hand she had seen so often raised from the podium in the beautiful extolling gestures to human worth and dignity, which did, of course, include her; and she was very ashamed of having shuddered. Professor Mephesto gave her knee a little squeeze before withdrawing his hand.

"It's an 'A' paper, my dear, an 'A-*plus*' paper. Absolutely top-drawer!"

Candy's heart gave a little leap. It was certainly a well-known fact that Professor Mephesto never allowed more than one "A-plus" paper to his entire class for any particular thesis.

"Thank you," she managed to breathe.

"I've no doubt," said Professor Mephesto gently, rising from his chair again, "that you are sincere." He frowned before continuing. "There are so many who profess noble beliefs and insights, without really *feeling* them."

He walked about the office as he spoke, pausing here and there to touch, in reverence, a book, or to raise a hand to emphasize his meaning.

"Very few people are capable of *feeling* things today—I suppose it is our commercial way of life; it has destroyed the capacity to *feel* . . . the *art* to feel—for it requires an artist . . . to *truly feel*. Yet talk is cheap. And that is, of course, what accounts for the pathetic failure of organized religion . . . the mere lip-service to the eternal values. Insincerity! A greater disservice to humankind could not be imagined!"

He stopped near the back of Candy's chair, where the girl sat, quite stiffly, staring ahead; she recalled seeing him with the other students, how relaxed and informal they had seemed together, and she made a tremendous effort to emulate their behavior by leaning back now in her chair and having another sip of the sherry, her mind meanwhile racing desperately through the pages she had read this term, trying to find something smart and appropriate to say. She could think of nothing however, for her mind was filled with the recurrent thought, A truly great man. I'm in the presence of a truly great man. And, as she heard behind her now the heavy breathing of the professor, she imagined that the sounds were just the same as those of a man in a story of long ago, after he had carried his burden up Calvary Hill. And she managed to subdue her impulse to flinch this time, when the professor laid his hand on her shoulder, and moved it then to the back of her neck.

"I really believe," he said gently, "that you have the . . . true insight, the true wisdom, the *true feeling*," pausing before he added . . . in a whisper, ". . . and I believe you know *my* great need of *you!*"

As he spoke he gradually slipped his hand around her neck, along her throat and toward her breast, and Candy dropped her glass of sherry.

"Oh, my goodness," she wailed, going forward at once from her chair to pick the pieces off the floor, for the glass had broken and scattered. She was so embarrassed she could scarcely speak for the moment.

"Oh, I'm sorry, I—"

"Never mind about that," said Professor Mephesto huskily, coming down beside her, "it's nothing, only a material object—the merest chimera of existence!"

On the floor next to her, he put his face to the back of her neck and one hand under her sweater.

"You won't deny me," he pleaded, "I know you are too wise and too good to be selfish. . . . Surely you meant what you wrote." And he began to quote urgently " '. . . the beautiful, thrilling privilege of giving fully,' " meanwhile pressing forward against her. But as he did, Candy sprang to her feet again and the professor lost his balance and fell sideways, rolling in the spilled sherry, trying to soften his fall with one hand and to pull the girl down with the other, but he failed in both these efforts; and now, having taken a nasty bump in the fall and, per- haps too, because of his unwieldy bulk, he merely lay for the moment in the pool of sherry, wallowing and groaning.

Candy was startled almost to alarm, standing now, one hand to her mouth.

"Oh, Professor Mephesto, I—"

"Comfort those whose needs are greatest, my dear," he implored her from where he lay, arms outstretched to take her fully would she but come to him. "Remember the 'thrilling privilege'!"

But the poor girl was too frightened, and still terribly upset about having broken the glass.

"Oh, I don't know—" she stammered, almost tearfully, "I—I'm so afraid—I only wish—"

She stopped short as the door burst open and in came the young sullen-faced boy who had so begrudgingly conveyed the invitation to her. His eyes went wild and his face pale as he looked from one to the other of them.

"Excuse *me!*" he said then haughtily and turned on his heel to leave.

"Wait, Holly!" cried the professor, struggling to his feet, "Wait . . . it's only—" He got up, brushing himself awkwardly; he was clearly embarrassed, and the boy meanwhile had stopped in the half-open door, waiting, indeed.

"*I'd* better be going," said the boy, when no further explanation came.

"No, no, Holly," said Professor Mephesto, collecting himself and coming to the boy. "Go into the inner office," he said firmly.

The boy looked at him, no longer pale now, sulky and dark.

"Go," repeated the professor; then he laid a hand on the boy's arm. "I'll go with you," he said gently, "come."

He turned to Candy just before closing the inner-office door. "Excuse us for a minute, please," he said.

"Yes, of course," said the bewildered girl, and she sat down again in the chair. For a moment she could hear the murmur of their voices, then something like a door slamming and she knew the young man had left. She waited a minute but the professor did not return. Selfish! Selfish! she was thinking of herself. To be needed by this great man! And to be only concerned with my material self! She was horribly ashamed. How he needs me! And I deny him! *I* deny *him!* Oh, how did I *dare?*

She listened, and her heart grew swollen and soft within her as she heard what was unmistakably a sob. "Oh Prof—" She could not bear it; he was alone, weeping in his need for her—"Oh, Meph, Meph," she started up, and toward the door. She would go to him, give herself to him—fully. She recalled the image of her nakedness in the glass as she had stepped from the bath this morning. Yes, she was lovely; she would give him that—fully. Fleetingly now, as she put her hand on the knob of the inner-office door, she wished that she had worn her finest underthings, but she knew with satisfaction that these were fresh and sweet. And then she heard another sob, a moan. "I'm coming, *Meph,*" she whispered, and softly opened the door.

But the young man had *not* left, and Candy was confronted with an extraordinary scene. The two of them were dancing about the clothes-strewn room, stark naked, flailing each other wildly with wet hand towels, moaning and sobbing, their bodies reddened and welted.

They didn't see her, or if they did, were not distracted, so intense their engagement as they lashed out in great frenzy. Candy closed the door quickly and rushed out of the office and down the long quiet hall, finally bursting into tears, only conscious now of her swift little footsteps, and of her terrible selfishness, how it had driven Professor Mephesto, in his frustration, to . . . goodness knows what! *"Oh, how could I?"* she kept demanding of herself. *"How could I?"*

By the time she reached home, however, she was more composed; at least she was eager to tell her father about the A-plus thesis she had done.

Mr. Christian was sitting in his armchair, reading the paper.

"Hi!" he said, glancing at his watch as she came in. "Have a nice day?" He knew enough to alternate his salutation from "Learn anything?" to "Have a nice day?" and he did this with clocklike regularity.

"Well," said Candy, coming forward to give him a kiss on the forehead, which he received with a grunt. "An *A-plus* on my last philosophy thesis! From Professor Mephesto! He never gives more than one for the whole class! Isn't it wonderful?"

Mr. Christian's questions were, of course, rhetorical, but so was his interest, so he could sustain the line of them easily enough.

"Oh?" he said, in slightly rising inflection, continuing to look at his paper, though with a frown which showed he was just scanning, and was, certainly, listening to his daughter too, "what was the *subject* of the thesis?"

" 'Contemporary Human Love,' " said Candy, putting her things away.

Mr. Christian shook his paper, clearing his throat.

"That sounds practical," he said. He tried to force a little laugh to show that philosophy courses weren't serious, but he was too basically ill-tempered to manage it, so he shook his paper again, clearing his throat and frowning a bit more darkly than before.

Candy ignored it; she was determined to salvage something of her triumph, and she wasn't going to let him spoil it.

"*And—*" she said, coming over to sit down near him, "I was invited to a conference with Professor Mephesto! To 'have a drop.'"

The name of Professor Mephesto had come up previously, and Mr. Christian loathed it with the most simple-minded unrestrained jealousy. He took his pipe and began to empty it vigorously against the nearest ashtray.

"What did *he* want?" he asked, in frank contempt.

"Oh, Daddy! Really! It's the greatest *honor* to be invited to Professor Mephesto's office, and have a drop! I've *told* you that a dozen times! Good Grief!"

"Have-a-drop-of-*what?*" asked Mr. Christian slowly, feigning the patience of a saint.

"Of sherry, of course! I *told* you that a hundred times!"

"Sherry *wine?*" asked her father, making his frown one great black hole.

"No, sherry banana-split! Silly! Of course, sherry wine! He has a glass of sherry and a bit of cheese in the afternoon—some people prefer tea, but others find tea lacking. Whereas sherry has body *and* edge, and tea is so messy at best, don't you . . . well, Good Grief, I mean it's a taste he acquired in the best possible circles!"

"And he gives this wine to *students?*" That was the big point with Mr. Christian.

"Oh, Daddy!"

Candy got up and walked over to the window. Where she had begun by feeling just slightly ambiguous about her conference with Mephesto, now she felt in it the strength and rightness of the world itself.

Mr. Christian puffed on his pipe.

"I simply want to know—"

"I don't wish to discuss it," said Candy, primly.

What was going on in her father's mind, behind that impossibly dark brow, it is difficult to convey in full. Certainly he was furious with her, strove to dominate her, would argue, sulk and yet not raise a hand against her. Did he know he was playing a losing game? And is it, moreover, too much to believe that he enjoyed, not simply losing the game, but being a *bad loser* as well? In any event, he immediately lunged upon another very sore point between them.

"Then perhaps you will discuss *this,*" he said, tight-lipped. "Mrs. Harris said you were talking to Emmanuel again yesterday."

Emmanuel was the Mexican boy who came to mow the lawn. Mr. Christian had strictly forbidden Candy to talk to him as she had shown, on a number of occasions, an inclination to do. Mr. Christian had said that he, personally, was broad-minded enough not to mind, but that it "looked funny" to the neighbors. He somehow associated the event with Professor Mephesto.

But for Candy this was the last straw.

"And I certainly *won't* discuss *that!*" she said. "I'm so

ashamed of you about *that* that I could die. Why, if Professor Mephesto knew that you had said that, I would *never* have been invited to his office! Not in a million years!"

Her father felt a severe, delicious pain in his head. It was with the greatest effort that he kept from blacking out, as he controlled his voice, and said:

"I don't like to have to cut down on your allowance, but—"

"My allowance!"

Candy stamped her foot in pique.

"My gosh, is that all you can ever think of? Material things? Good Grief!"

With a toss of her pretty head, she turned abruptly, marched out of the room and up the stairs to her bed.

In the living room behind her, Mr. Christian looked back down at his paper, puffed on his pipe, and slowly, stiffly, shook his head, his lips and knuckles now the color of snow.

And that night Candy went to sleep trying to decide which she should do: give herself to the Mexican gardener, or run away to New York City.

three

3

The next day was Saturday, and Candy had no classes; she didn't get up until about ten. When she went downstairs, Mr. Christian had already left for the office, as he usually did on Saturday mornings, to "take care of a few things that have been piling up."

Candy always enjoyed having breakfast alone, for then she could drink her coffee undisturbed by her father's frown and his occasional quips about "cocoa being best for a growing girl." This morning she had two cups, from time to time looking anxiously out the breakfast-nook window, into the sunny backyard—for this was the day that Emmanuel came to mow. And Candy had made her decision.

After her coffee and toast (she told herself she was much too excited to have more) she went back upstairs to her bath, and afterwards put on one of her prettiest summer dresses, and a touch of her favorite perfume, Tabu. Then she went downstairs and out the back door.

She found Emmanuel, kneeling at one of the flower beds at the side of the house, turning the earth with a trowel. How thin and wan he looked in his poor clothes. Oh, thought Candy, he does need me so *very* much!

"Hi!" she said brightly.

Emmanuel looked up, somewhat surprised to see her.

"Ha," he said. He did not speak English too well.

"That doesn't look like much fun," said Candy, referring to his work.

"Whot?"

He frowned up at her; from the beginning of their conversations he had thought she was the dumbest girl he had ever met.

"Wouldn't you like to come inside for a drink of something cool?" asked Candy, showing her white teeth and wet pink tongue in a silvery laugh.

"I don thunk Mister Christy wud leek," said the gardener at last when he had understood her proposal.

"Oh, darn Daddy, anyway," said Candy. "Surely I can entertain friends in my own home occasionally without *his* making a fuss!" But, of course, she knew he was right; so it was finally agreed, through a series of repetitions and gestures, that the gardener would go ahead of her into the garage and she would join him there with the drinks.

When she reached the garage she found him kneeling again, this time sharpening the blades of the lawn mower.

"How devoted you are!" said Candy, beaming, "I should think you could find something better to do on a lovely day like this!"

"Whot?"

She handed him the drink, bringing herself very close as

she did, so that he could not fail to feel her warmth, nor to catch the fragrance of her Tabu.

"It's a drop of sherry," she said, at the same time indicating a box for them to sit on, "I think you'll like it."

"Whot?"

When they were seated, the gardener understood for perhaps the first time, when he had a tentative sip of the wine, what was being offered him.

"This good!" he said with a broad smile at the glass.

"Yes," said Candy, "I find it has body *and* edge. Not like tea, a messy affair at best. Don't you agree?"

"Whot?"

"Now then," she said, hurrying on, for beneath her composure, the girl was quite excited, "tell me about yourself —your values, your plans and aspirations; tell me all sorts of things about yourself."

"Whot?"

"Oh, Emmanuel," said Candy with a soft sigh and a look that had become mournful, "it's so very difficult for you here, isn't it?"

She put her hand on his arm, closing her eyes, and leaning forward as though to comfort him in her understanding—and with some satisfaction she felt her breast touch against the back of his arm. She was all prepared to be kissed violently, but when it did not come, she opened her eyes to see the gardener staring at her oddly, suspiciously. For a moment she was flushed with confusion, which she covered by saying:

"Emmanuel, *look* at me. Listen to me now," she continued in a grave tone, taking his hands in her own, "I know you don't think Daddy—Mr. Christian—likes you.

But I want you to know that we aren't all like that, I mean that *all* human beings aren't like that! Do you understand? Nothing is so beautiful as the human face." Her manner had become quite severe, indeed, almost intimidating, and the gardener watched her with eyes grown large in wonder.

"You know, don't you," the girl went on, softer now, "that *I'm* not like that—that I'm *very* fond of you," and she leaned forward again, closed-eyed, to his face and finally to his mouth, kissing him, deeply, and upsetting their glasses of sherry. And Candy was prepared to tell him not to bother about that, a material object of no importance, but it was not necessary, for with a few whimpering sounds of surprise, the gardener had held her kiss and was reaching into her dress now for her breast while his other hand had plunged between her legs.

"Oh, my darling," Candy was saying. "You do need me so, you do need me so!"

But it was happening much faster than the girl had planned, and she became truly frightened now, as he tore at her small white panties, trying, with considerable urgency, to remove them.

"Oh darling, please, not here, not now, we mustn't," and she quickly broke away from him and ran to the door of the garage, where he followed her and renewed his attack, so that the girl rushed out into the open and the skirmish persisted halfway across the backyard.

Finally she calmed him, near the rhododendrons.

"Tonight," she promised in a whisper. "Come to me at midnight," and she indicated her bedroom, which was directly above them. "Oh I know how you need me, my darling," she said, pressing her pelvis against his leg, "and

I do so want it to be *perfect* for us. Come to my bedroom at midnight," she said again, stealing away, one hand outstretched to him as she went in the back door—and a good thing, too, for Daddy Christian's big Plymouth was just pulling in the drive at that very moment.

That evening at dinner, Mr. Christian was unfolding his napkin as he asked, frowning seriously:

"Have a good day?"

"So-so," said Candy, toying with the cottage cheese and peach salad before her and avoiding her father's eyes.

"Hmm," he said, "nothing wrong, is there?"

"Oh, no," said the girl lazily, "no, no."

"Hmm," said Mr. Christian. He cleared his throat. "Well, Aunt Ida wants us to come over for Sunday dinner tomorrow."

Candy continued eating.

"I don't know whether we should go or not," said her father in a controlled voice. "I mean, there's not much point in going if you're just going to sulk all the time."

She glared at him furiously, while he cleared his throat, seeming more at ease now that he had roused her anger.

"Well," he went on, "I mean, if you're in one of your *moods,* we don't want to inflict it on Aunt Ida and the others, do we? There's not much point in that, is there?"

"As far as I'm concerned," said Candy sharply, "there's not much point in *anything* around here!"

And she left the table in a huff.

Mr. Christian gave his exasperation-sigh and went on with his peach salad, unable to keep his fork from shaking a little, but managing, with certain effort, not to drive it suddenly into his chest.

four

4

At eleven-thirty that night, Candy had another bath—a bubble bath this time steeped with pine-fragrance crystals —and put on the black nightgown she had bought for the occasion. Finally, a fresh application of Tabu, and, by five minutes to midnight, she was in her bed, the lamp a glowing rose, and soft music purring from the radio.

Mr. Christian's room was at the far end of the hall, so she was not overly anxious about his being disturbed—and the idea of giving herself to the Mexican gardener right under his nose was not without a certain excitement itself; in fact, in one sense, that was more or less the whole point.

Promptly at midnight Emmanuel arrived, entering across the roof and through Candy's window as they had planned. Candy lay stretched on the bed, the veritable picture of provocation, her blond hair spread like golden flames across the silken rose-lit pillow, and the black shimmering nightgown clinging to her body which lay with a slight reptilian curve, lush at the breast and thigh, lithe and willowy along the waist and limbs.

The gardener stared in amazement; it was too much like a movie or a folktale for him to fully believe, as the lovely girl stretched out her arms, half closed-eyed, whispering:

"Darling, I knew you would come."

He was dressed as he had been earlier in the day; and still wearing his sneakers, he made no noise as he crossed the carpeted floor to the bed and took the girl in his arms.

"Undress quickly, my darling," Candy breathed, "and don't make a sound." She put a finger to her lips and made her eyes wide to emphasize the necessity of this.

Emmanuel was in the bed in a trice, embracing her feverishly, and snatching her gown at once up to her shoulders.

"Oh, you do need me so!" the closed-eyed girl murmured, as yet not feeling much of anything except the certainty of having to fit this abstraction to the case. But when the gardener's hand closed on her pelvis and into the damp, she stiffened slightly: she was quite prepared to undergo *pain* for him . . . but *pleasure*—she was not sure how that could be a part of the general picture. So she seized his hand and contented herself for the moment with the giving of her left breast, to which his mouth was fastened in desperate sucking.

"Oh my baby, my baby," she whispered, stroking his head; but the hot insulting hardness of him between her legs was distracting, and somehow destroyed the magic of her breast sacrifice. She closed her eyes again and called upon Professor Mephesto's words; 'The needs of man are so *many* . . . and so *aching*.' "Oh how you ache for me, my darling!" She flung both arms around his neck, as he found her tiny clitoris and pummeled it with his calloused fingers, causing her to cry out and stiffen once more in his arms; but now she fought down the desire to seize his hand, thinking how this was the price of loveliness and the key to the beautiful thrilling privilege of giving fully—and so the gardener would have entered her then, with a terrible thrust to the hilt, so to speak . . . had not a padded scurrying sounded at that moment in the hall.

"Good Grief," cried Candy, in a very odd voice, "it's Daddy!" pushing her hands violently against the gardener's chest. "It's *Daddy!*"

And true enough, the door burst open at that instant and Mr. Christian appeared, looking like some kind of giant insane lobster-man. At the sight of them he reeled, his face going purple, then hatefully black, as he crashed sideways against the wall, smashed back by the sheer impact of the spectacle itself. It was not as though he couldn't believe his eyes, for it was a scene that had formed a part of many many of his most lively and hideous dreams—dreams which began with Candy being *ravished*, first by Mephesto, then by foreigners, then by Negroes, then gorillas, then bulldogs, then donkeys, horses, mules, kangaroos, elephants, rhinos, and finally, in the grand finale, by all of them at once, grouped around different parts of her, though it was (in the finale) *she* who was the aggressor, *she* who was voraciously ravishing *them*, frantically forcing the bunched and spurting organs into every orifice—vagina, anus, mouth, ears, nose, etc. He had even dreamed once that she asked him if it were true that there was a small uncovered opening in the *pupil of the eye,* because if it were, she had said, she would have room there (during the finale) for a miniscule organ, like that of a praying mantis to enter her as well! So that now, actually confronted by the scene, one would think he was not unprepared, yet as dreams of death do not prepare a young man for the firing squad, but perhaps only build to the terrible intensity of it, so Mr. Christian appeared now to be actually strangling with shock.

"*. . . urg . . . ack . . . chchch,*" were the sounds he produced for the first moment as he clawed at the air in front of him; then he came toward them like a man on stilts, picking up a chair and raising it stiffly over his head.

"Daddy!" cried Candy in real alarm, but it was too late, for he swung the chair down at Emmanuel, who was leaping from the bed; it missed him and shattered against the bedpost. But he still retained a leg of the chair, and this, as a club, was a more formidable weapon than the chair itself, as he came relentlessly forward after the gardener, managing at last to speak through his grating teeth:

"*You . . . You . . . You . . .* COMMUNIST!"

He swung repeatedly at the gardener's head, making little cries of repulsion, as might a woman in having to kill a snake with a stick, and hitting instead in his blind fury the bedroom wall, again and again; but there was no escape for the gardener. Yet he was not prepared to die, and whimpering like a trapped animal he dived for his pile of clothes, near the bed . . . for it was among them that he had left his *trowel,* which he managed to recover in a scuttling frenzy and to raise on high—as Mr. Christian lunged in for the kill—and then, before making his getaway, to plunge it with a cry more of fear than of triumph, right down through the top of Mr. Christian's black, splitting headache.

five

5

"Oh Daddy, Daddy, poor Daddy," Candy was saying at his bedside in the Municipal Hospital a day later. By virtue of one of the most extraordinary wounds ever received or administered in Racine County, Mr. Christian was not dead, but had suffered a partial lobotomy when the trowel had entered his cranium. Now, he was half sitting in bed, his head swathed in a great hulking bandage, an expression of complete repose on his face.

"Now, don't worry, kitten, he's going to be *all right*," Candy's Uncle Jack assured the girl, standing close beside her, stroking her shoulder comfortingly, "he's going to be *all right*."

Candy squeezed his hand in her own, as though it were he who needed comforting, "Oh yes, Uncle Jack," she agreed softly, "I *know* that he is."

Uncle Jack Christian was her father's twin brother. They looked exactly alike, though Jack somehow seemed much younger, more alive to the feelings and needs of her own generation—at least, that was what Candy had often told herself, and her father, too. Before his marriage, he and Candy had been *pals,* and they continued to be very close, and when together engaged in a good deal of innocent, pawing affection—rather to the annoyance of Mr. Christian—though they did not see much of each other now because Candy's father took such strong objection to his brother's vivacious wife, Livia, and considered her a bad influence on Candy.

"Now, why don't we go have some tea with your Aunt Livia?" Uncle Jack suggested. "Or perhaps you'd prefer a drink—I know I could use one."

Like Professor Mephesto, Uncle Jack was one of Candy's heroes, too.

"Yes, I *could* use a drink," she said gravely.

Aunt Livia was waiting for them in the car. She was so lovely and sophisticated that she had always intimidated Candy, whom she treated either like a child of three, or at other times, like a woman of the world, as she talked lightly of adultery, homosexuality and other things which Candy's father would never dream of mentioning, not in a million years.

"How is he?" she said, twinkling.

"Well, he took a pretty nasty knock, of course," said Uncle Jack seriously, after he had held the door open for Candy and then seated himself beside his wife.

"Knock?" said Aunt Livia, looking all around in surprise, "I thought it was a *gouge,* or something like that. After all, isn't a *trowel* a—"

Uncle Jack cleared his throat (he was his brother's

brother all right, even so). "Yes, well, he's much better now; he's resting."

"That's nice," said Aunt Livia, quite sincerely. Then she began to laugh. *"Knock!* You poor idiot! What you don't know about the English language—" and she laughed so hard that she finally began to cough.

"Well, really, Liv," Uncle Jack protested, "I should think that some things—"

"Doesn't matter," said Aunt Livia, waving him desist. "Live and learn." Then she was distracted. "My God, look at that pregnant woman on the corner there—she's going to have that baby before the light changes! Good God, did you ever see anything like that? If I look another moment I shall vomit all over us!"

She turned around to Candy, who was in the back seat.

"How are you, my dear?" she asked, as though she hadn't noticed her before. *"You* aren't pregnant, I hope?"

"N-O spells *no,*" said Candy with as much dignity as she could master. She didn't like to be with Aunt Livia when she was in one of her 'clever moods,' as Uncle Jack called them. And she felt that Uncle Jack was especially misunderstood at those times. In many ways, Candy regretted the marriage as much as her father did. On the other hand, Aunt Livia *could* be perfectly charming, and often was.

"Well, I must say, you're certainly looking lovely, Candy," she went on, appraising the girl closely.

"Thank you," said Candy, flushing deeply.

"Have any of the boys gotten into those little white pants of yours yet?" Aunt Livia asked, as though she were speaking of the weather.

"*Really*, Liv," said Uncle Jack, coughing, "this hardly seems the appro—"

"But, isn't she *lovely?*" his wife persisted, turning to Jack Christian, "a ripe little piece she's getting to be, I'd say. It seems to me that's the first question that would occur to anyone! Though I suppose you haven't noticed! Well, perhaps *you* wouldn't!" she added, and began to laugh again, sustaining it for a moment while the other two looked out the window uneasily. "Oh God, haven't we come far enough," she went on then in a change of mood, "let's have a drink."

"Right," said Jack Christian, "I could *use* one. How about you, Can?"

" '*Can*'?" echoed his wife, laughing wildly again. "That isn't *all* she could use either—is it, 'Can'?"

"Now, Liv," objected Uncle Jack, "I'm sure we don't know what you mean by that, and—well, here we are at Halfway House," he turned in then at a large broad drive leading up to a luxury roadhouse, "and now for a drink, eh girls?" he added cheerfully.

"Right," said Liv, "out of these wet pants and into a dry martini! Eh, 'Can'?" And she gave the blushing girl a suggestive wink.

"Liv's in one of her moods," Uncle Jack explained to Candy as he helped her out of the car.

"I'll say!" said Candy.

"I'm in the mood for cock and plenty of it!" cried Liv gaily. "About ten pounds, please, thick and fast!"

"Now, Liv, this won't do," said Uncle Jack firmly, as, with a gracious sweep, he bade them through the wide portals of Halfway House.

They were a handsome party and, to all appearances,

as wholesome a representation of middle-class innocence as had even been in Halfway House; the *maître d'hôtel* came forward with a flourish and secured them a choice table.

"What about a bite to eat, as well, girls?" asked Uncle Jack, genially looking over the menu while the waiter hovered at hand.

"Yes, a bit of giant Male Organ—piping hot!" quipped Liv, scrutinizing the menu with a frown.

"Now, Liv," said Uncle Jack, laying down his menu gently, "you *will* go too far."

"Who's talking about 'go'?" demanded Liv. "The girls want to *come!* Am I right, Can?"

Candy blushed crimson, and Uncle Jack sighed and shrugged a look of bemused patience at the waiter, who, though fidgeting about, managed to smile uneasily.

"Oh bother," said Liv, flinging down her menu, "I'll just have a drink. Drink now, organ later!"

"Right," said Jack, "three martinis, please. Rather dry."

"Well," he continued when the waiter had left, looking casually about the crowded room, "nice gathering today at Halfway House. Have you been here before, Candy? Rather cleverly appointed, I think, for this sort of thing, eh? Do you like it at all?"

"Oh yes," the girl began, "I think it's—"

"Sometimes I think I can almost come by just *looking* at something!" exclaimed Liv in sudden good spirits. "That knife and spoon, for instance. Why, I've only to give my clit a tiny flick right now and I'd be sopping!"

"I wish you wouldn't, Liv," said Uncle Jack, speaking plainly.

"Well, it *isn't* too likely, is it?" asked his wife, looking at him in wonder. "I mean how on earth could I? Oh, I suppose I could pretend to drop something in my lap, and then—"

"I *mean* to say," said Uncle Jack deliberately, "that I wish you wouldn't *talk* in that way—"

"I'm going to keep a little clothespin on my clit and then I can pinch it if I want!" said Liv, and she burst out laughing. "Did you ever think of doing that, Can?"

"N-O," said Candy, "spells *no!*" It annoyed and confused her for Aunt Livia to talk this way, and she sympathized greatly with her Uncle Jack's having to endure it. Fortunately the awkward tension was broken at that moment by the appearance of a well-dressed elderly couple entering the door.

"I say," said Uncle Jack, brightening suddenly, "isn't that Mr. and Mrs. Edward Kingsley who've just come in—yes, of course it is! I *wonder* if they wouldn't join us for a drink," and so saying he rose and caught the matronly lady's eye, and they exchanged hearty salutations.

"Jack Christian!" said Mrs. Kingsley, coming over to him. "How delicious to see you!" and she allowed herself to be seated. "And Livia, too! How are you, my dear!"

Mr. and Mrs. Kingsley were extremely proper, if one may judge by appearances and deportment, and while Mr. Christian and Mr. Kingsley remained standing for the moment, waiting for additional chairs to be brought, they were introduced to Candy, and Mr. Christian was able to caution his wife in a whisper: "Best behavior, dear. You know what this account means to us!" But it would seem, for the moment at least, that Uncle Jack's apprehensions on this point were unfounded, because Liv's mood had changed quite abruptly; and after the two gentlemen were seated, and all had fresh drinks, conversation became pleasant and general, finally turning to art, and at last to the drama of stage and cinema.

"How very interesting!" Liv was saying after Mr. Kingsley had expressed his serious regret that so little of "real worth" was being done in the new medium of television. "For, as a matter of fact," she continued, "a friend of mine is toying just now with a thing which *could* develop into something really top-drawer—if he can find the capital to back it. Perhaps you'd be interested in hearing a little about it, Mr. Kingsley." She paused then to delve in her purse and extract a couple of folded sheets.

"Yes, certainly," said Mr. Kingsley, clearing his throat, "I'm always happy to invest in a . . . a really *good thing.*"

"Yes," said Liv, unfolding her papers, "well, I'll just read a bit of this outline—it *might* be exactly what you're looking for." And so she proceeded to read from the paper, maintaining a very serious expression, and only raising her voice to make points of emphasis, or when it seemed that Uncle Jack wished to interrupt her:

"It's called, *They Met in the Park,* and it's the parallel stories of two young minds damaged by war. We fade in on a slow sweep-shot over the expansive grounds of the Los Angeles V.A. Hospital. As the camera moves forward in a wide-angle pan of the estate, the music is up in a montage-medley of service tunes—the 'Marine Hymn,' 'Caissons Go Rolling Along,' the 'Air Corps Song,' etc.—a sort of mosaic *musicale* which builds to a rousing crescendo of 'Anchors Away' sung by a choir of 200 eleven-year-old boys. As we approach the hospital, the dedication is narrated in a fine voice (perhaps Senator Dirksen's)—something about sacrifice, endeavor, etc., on the part of the nurses and doctors of the Veterans' Hospitals 'throughout this great land of ours . . . this *America*.' As the music fades to a muted and distant 'Taps,' the camera zeroes into a private ward (one of countless thousands—that's the feeling here—but still a little something special about this 'typical' case). An air of solemnity prevails in the room. Two doctors are standing by the single bed. The senior doctor is looking at the patient's chart, very thoughtfully. His younger colleague stands by, watching the other's face with reverence and restrained anticipation. Finally, the senior doctor speaks, decisively: 'Yes, Doctor, we'll begin shock-therapy *today!*'

"The patient is suffering from battle-fatigue and has lost every faculty except the sense of smell. Each time he regains consciousness, he begins frantically running his fingers between his toes and then smelling them, trying to force them up his nose, etc. They always have to give him a sedative to keep him from disfiguring himself. By way of making it perfectly *clear* as to the momentous task involved in one of these thankless jobs, the beginning treatments are shown to fail, and the entire first half of the play (it runs for an hour—I had in mind the *U.S. Steel Hour*) is comprised of successive scenes in which the two doctors are standing by the patient's bed, waiting to see how he will act when he again regains consciousness. Each time, one of them turns to the other and says, not without a touch of quiet anxiety, 'He's coming around, Doctor!' The camera pans from the senior doctor's face, to the younger's, back to the senior's, then down to the patient as he regains consciousness, opening his eyes, staring blankly for a moment before giving a savage grunt and starting wildly for his toes —whereupon, the elder doctor frowns darkly and says, 'Doctor, give the patient a sedative!' This identical two-minute scene is repeated fifteen times. Finally, the patient is pronounced well. (The pronouncement comes during the halfway commercial break and is not actually known to anyone who hasn't read the script.)

"The opening scene, after the break, is in a smart rest clinic in the French Alps. For the furnishings of this set no expense should be spared, no detail overlooked, to authenticate the desired mood—gracious living. The room is light and airy, the appointments exquisitely delicate. A very large picture-window affords a mountain panorama, a vista of rose-white snow, and sky the color of blue smoke.

"On the bed, clad in a peignoir of topaz Chantilly, lies a girl patient. As the scene opens, her physician has just entered:

> DR. HERSHOLT:
> (*pleasantly*)

Well, Bambi! And how do we feel this morning, eh?

> BAMBI:
> (*frowning*)

What?

> DR. HERSHOLT:
> (*tentatively*)

Well, I mean . . . uh . . . you know . . . how . . . do . . .

BAMBI:

(*interrupting*)

Doctor, I had a dream last night—it's been puzzling me ever since. (*She looks puzzled, cute*) I mean, dreams *do* have secret meanings . . . *don't* they?

DR. HERSHOLT:

(*seriously*)

Yes, child, very often they do. (*Then in genuine interest*) Now, why don't you tell us about it?

BAMBI:

(*after a sigh*)

Well, I dreamed I was in a big place—it reminded me somehow of my house . . . at home, in Glendale. And my father was there with me . . . always . . . we were together . . . alone. And I . . . I kept sucking him off. (*She looks puzzled, cute*) What does the dream *mean*, Doctor?

"There is another commercial break here which blots out the doctor's reply. The next scene opens in a crowded elevator of a New York office building in Columbus Circle. The camera pans down from above during the elevator's descent, then cuts to the foyer where an elevator (a different one) is opening and a crowd of people issue forth. Among them is Bambi. She leaves the building and starts walking across Central Park. Near the lake she is attacked by a husky chap. He throws her to the ground, has her securely pinioned, and (it is the patient!) begins grappling wildly at her feet, smelling them, trying to force them up his nose, etc. A passing policeman (played by Edmond Lowe) sees the tomfoolery and rushes them with his stick.

He drives the patient away with blows to the head and shoulders. He chases him for some distance, into the lake (there is an underwater fight scene, etc.). When the policeman gets back to Bambi, he finds she is furious—writhing around on the ground, seething with rage, frothing, groveling, etc. 'I wanted a piece of that husky chap!' she cries. 'Suck! Fuck! Shit! Piss! Cunt! Cock! Crap!' She is very cross. The policeman starts hitting at her with his stick—as he would a snake. 'Your *stick*' she cries then, ignoring the blows. 'GIVE ME YOUR STICK!'

"Camera fades out slowly and into a Bellevue ward. It is a month later. Bambi sits in a wheelchair, stricken with paralysis. Ever since the attack, she has not been able to walk. Her doctor (played by Huntz Hall) believes it is psychosomatic. In one of his lines to his assistant (played by George Arliss) he says, 'The girl has apparently lost the *will-to-walk*.' Arliss replies, 'I don't get you *at all,* Doc,' which gives rise to some smart banter and repartee, a nifty five-minute *jeu-de-mots* between Hall and Arliss on words like 'walk,' 'work,' 'wouk,' etc. This will be the first time Hall and Arliss have worked together, and we may expand that scene so it will come across as a sort of leitmotif of the whole, or else use it in bits, as filler, in the scenes that have profanity in them—which is about the *knottiest* problem we're up against with this getting this piece on the boards.

"To conclude, there are seven identical scenes which show Hall trying to coax Bambi out of her wheelchair. There is no dialogue in these scenes; they simply show Hall standing on one side of the room and beckoning to Bambi. The background music for these scenes is 'Lover Man,' played as though under water, by Lee Konitz. The curtain scene is not too bad. It shows Hall leaning against the window, trying to shoot some dope into the vein of his temple. There is a scuffling noise in the background; he drops his spike and turns. It's Bambi, holding out her arms and walking slowly toward him. There is a smile on her face as she says, 'Look, Doctor, I can . . . COME!' "

Aunt Livia sat quietly when she had finished her reading, frowning down at the paper as though it were something not wholly satisfactory. "Of course, it wants more work," she said, "a few wrinkles to be ironed out, some tightening up, brightening up, et cetera, but the first question is *capital*—how about it, Eddie, can I put you down for a few thousand?"

"I *think* we had better be going," said Mrs. Kingsley in a grand manner. She seemed quite offended by the recitation as a whole. Mr. Kingsley was more ambivalent. He did not seem to think much of the project's chances, and was quick to say so, in so many words, but on the other hand he was somewhat excited by the beauty of the girls—Aunt Livia and Candy—and the fact that one of them was involved in the arts in any way at all *did* intrigue him.

"There's a question here," he said, fumbling momentarily for the right word, ". . . of . . . of *taste,* and I find myself wondering if . . . if . . ."

Mrs. Kingsley rose to her feet abruptly.

"You may remain here and be made a fool of, if you wish, Edward," she said, "that is *your* affair. For my part, I am leaving immediately!" But before she left, she indicated Candy with a nod and said to Aunt Livia, with genuine feeling:

"That your remarks may be a distasteful annoyance to adults is unfortunate, but that this lovely child should be exposed . . . to the eruptions of a . . . a *sick* mind . . . is not simply distasteful—it is *criminal!*" Whereupon Aunt Livia stuck out her tongue at the lady, and said: "Not so distasteful, I daresay, as your fat *clit!*" And Mrs. Kingsley shuddered visibly and strode away.

"I'm afraid you'll have to excuse me," said her husband, scrambling to his feet, making a quick bow to those at the table and hurrying out the door after Mrs. Kingsley.

Uncle Jack sighed deeply, shaking his head.

"Well, I can't help but feel that was a mistake, Liv," he said gloomily, "after all, they aren't in arts, you can hardly expect them to share your—"

"Perhaps," said Livia, putting her papers away, "perhaps *not*. It may have quite excited Mrs. Kingsley though, you see. It's very hard to know exactly what is taking place in her mind. Certain images may remain, and—oh, I don't think old Kingsley will sink any money into it, if that's what you mean. No, if my guess is any good, he's more interested in getting into my *pants*, or our little niece's here, because—"

"That is *not my* meaning at all, Liv!" said Uncle Jack tersely. "Must you always mistake my meaning? What I mean to say is, quite simply, that you most probably have spoiled my chance with the Kingsleys for renewal of the Allerton contract! As I've told you time and time again, Mr. Kingsley is their representative in the matter, and the question has come up recently about—"

"Oh dear, really," protested Aunt Liv, "must you talk shop *twenty-four hours a day!* Good Lord!" She looked away haughtily, and it was quite clear that she was annoyed. "If you've no concern for me, you might at least think of our guest—spare her the boredom of such affairs!"

"Yes, of course," said Uncle Jack, turning his attention to Candy, "I'm afraid we've been neglecting you, my dear." He gave her slender hand a little pat. "What about another drink?"

"Oh no," said Candy, a bit dazed by it all, "I simply couldn't. I think I'd better get back to the hospital and see if Daddy needs anything."

"Right," said Uncle Jack. "Well, one for the road, and we're off."

In the car, it was decided that they would drop Aunt Livia at home—since she insisted she had "several affairs" to tend—and then Uncle Jack would drive Candy back to the hospital.

When they reached the hospital, Jack said:

"I'll just come up with you for a minute to see how he's getting along."

"What about Aunt Livia?" asked Candy, rather petulantly, "I mean, won't she be waiting for you at home?"

Uncle Jack didn't answer at once.

"I imagine you find Liv rather trying at times, don't you, my dear?" he said instead.

"Well, I don't know how *you* can bear it sometimes," admitted Candy. "She doesn't seem to understand you at all . . . your needs, and . . . and . . ."

"Quite right," said Jack, reaching into the glove compartment and taking out a flask. "I could do with a bracer before seeing your father," he said. "Here, you'd better have one yourself."

"Oh no," said Candy, "I couldn't."

"Right," said Uncle Jack, having another. "Good girl!" He gave her a little kiss on the cheek. This pleased Candy, for they had not been very affectionate together since his marriage to Livia. And, in fact, Candy was a little jealous. "Well, I'll just take this flask along in case," he added, "—better safe than sorry, I've always said."

It was quite dark when they reached Mr. Christian's room, but they found him just as they had left him, half sitting up, staring straight ahead.

There was only one chair in the room, so Candy sat on that and her Uncle Jack sat on the floor, leaning on one elbow, taking occasional sips from his flask.

They sat without speaking for a long time, but finally Uncle Jack put his head down on the floor and dozed off. When Candy noticed, she came down beside him and tried to wake him up, gently, saying:

"Uncle Jack . . . Uncle Jack. You mustn't go to sleep here, on the floor, you'll take cold."

He stirred, reaching out to her with one arm.

"Oh, let me just be here a moment," he said, "Liv never lets me sleep."

"Be here *with* me, sweetheart," he added imploringly. It was the first time he had used the old name he had always called her before his marriage, and it almost brought tears to Candy's eyes.

"Oh you poor darling," she murmured, pressing close to him.

"Yes, give me your warmth," he said in hushed urgency, "how I need your warmth! Liv is so cold."

"Oh my poor darling," said Candy as he nestled his head between her breasts and pressed her closer.

"Give me your true warmth," he said, raising her sweater and her brassiere and taking her breast in his mouth.

In the lamplight her Uncle Jack's face was exactly like that of her father's, a fact which could hardly have escaped Candy as she watched him, nursing, stroking his head and sighing, "Oh my poor darling, oh my poor baby."

Meanwhile Uncle Jack's hands were not idle, but had found their way beneath her skirt and along her legs into the sweetening damp.

"Give me all your true warmth," he said, one hand fondling her tiny clitoris, the other pulling down her white panties.

"All my true warmth," breathed Candy, "oh how you need my warmth, my baby," and she lay very still while he undressed her and then himself; but when he thrust himself into her, forgetting her taut hymen, the girl cried out, and apparently this was overheard by the nurse in the corridor—because she rushed in at that moment, flinging the door open wide and shrieking in horror at the sight of these two, stark naked, hunching wildly half beneath the sickbed.

"Great God!" she screamed. "Have you no *shame!* Have you no *shame!*"

A husky woman, quite six feet tall and heavily built, the nurse threw herself against the pair who were writhing in oblivion.

"Great God!" she kept shouting. "Great God!" And through her raging strength and the tumultuous abandon of the lovers, the bed overturned, and all four—the fourth being Mr. Christian himself—were sprawling together in a heap.

"Good Grief!" cried Candy, in genuine alarm. "It's *Daddy!*"

The confusion was compounded by the fact that the bed-clothes and mattress had tumbled on top of the group—all, that is, except Mr. Christian, who had scrambled clear at the last instant.

He stood, smiling benevolently, and stared at the mattress as it heaved and bumped about wildly, with now a foot, now a muffled exclamation escaping from beneath . . .

It would be difficult to determine what he thought of this unusual spectacle; but surely *some* idea formed in his disabled mind for, after a few seconds, he went and gathered up the clothes of Uncle Jack, which lay strewn about the room, and then opened the door and disappeared into the corridor.

A moment later Candy herself emerged, panting, and pink with humiliation. She had but one idea—to run, to fly from this ignominious situation before it continued a second longer.

She had her skirt and sweater on in a jiffy. Never! she thought, slipping out the doorway. No, never! . . . It couldn't . . . it simply *never* could have happened!

The mattress went on plunging up and down for a time —and then, propelled by a particularly severe jolt, it flew off to the side. Beneath the sheets and blankets though, the struggle continued as furiously as ever. The reason for this was that Uncle Jack, half-buried in the bedding, had somehow fastened on to the nurse, thinking she was Candy.

"Your *warmth!*" he cried, unaware of his fatal error. "Give me your *warmth!*" Gripped tightly between his legs he held the nurse's upper arm which, because of its corpulence, he took to be Candy's thigh. "Now! Now *give me all your* WARMTH!" he gasped as he strove through the final ineffable seconds of his ecstasy.

Powerful as she was, the big woman could not dislodge her arm from that viselike clamp. She did, however, manage to catch hold of a metallic object which was on the floor (a brass bedpan) with her free arm and, by dint of crashing it repeatedly and hysterically on the head of her ravisher she finally succeeded—the straining muscles of Uncle Jack's legs suddenly went slack and let her go.

Once she had gotten to her feet the nurse quickly regained her professional efficiency. She righted the bed, replaced the mattress and bedding, and then, with a lusty heave, she lifted Uncle Jack—not doubting for a moment that he was Mr. Christian—set him in it and put his nightgown back on him.

Having tidied up and satisfied her sense of order, she paused and looked about the room. She was not at all certain what had happened . . . surely there had been a girl fornicating with—with the patient . . . but where was she?

One thing was evident: the patient's head was bleeding and would have to be dressed immediately. She sighed heavily and gave a last, brief glance to her assailant before going to get the gauze and antiseptic.

Though unconscious, the patient's smile—the same sweet smile as before—fashioned his mouth and illumined his face, rather angelically.

six

6

Next morning Candy stepped out of the shower's biting embrace, now feeling fresh and restored after a sound sleep; she slipped on her bathrobe and hurried down to get breakfast.

Before starting her toast and coffee, she turned on *The Sunrise Symphony*, a morning program of recorded music. Soon she heard the disquieting chords of Bartok's *Miraculous Mandarin Suite*.

"Darn!" she said, realizing she'd missed the nerve-shattering introduction and the hideously discordant section where the elderly sex pervert is murdered by gangsters.

The orchestra was just finishing the formless waltz of the syphilitic prostitute as Candy was putting bread in the toaster, and it was about to begin the anguished cacophonies of the scene where the old mandarin is stabbed and strangled, when the telephone rang. . . .

"Hello?" (It was Aunt Livia's voice.) "Is Uncle Jack there?"

"Oh!" Candy said, feeling very confused and embarrassed. She had succeeded in putting the previous day's events out of mind and now, at the sound of Livia's voice, it spilled back in untidily—all of it—the scene at Halfway House with the Kingsleys, the visit to the hospital . . . Oh, why had she done it! . . . But Uncle Jack's need of her had been so great, so—so *aching*. . . .

"Would you mind putting your Uncle Jack on the phone!" said Livia.

"Why, Aunt Livia, whatever are you talking about?" Candy asked in real, almost relieved, bewilderment.

"Well, I just happened to notice that my husband didn't come home last night," said Aunt Livia with heavy sarcasm, "and for some strange reason I thought he might be in *your bed!*"

"*Uncle Jack?* Do you mean *Uncle Jack?*"

"That's right. *Uncle Jack!*"

With a loud click the golden slices sprang up in the toaster, one of them jumping right out and tumbling on the floor.

"But—but what makes you think he's *here?*" Candy said, nervously picking the toast up from the floor.

"*Put him on the phone!*" Aunt Livia demanded.

"Now, Aunt Livia, there's no need to—"

"Cut the crap!" she thundered.

"But Uncle Jack isn't here I tell you! He *isn't here!*"

For a few seconds there was silence, as if Aunt Livia was digesting this information. Finally she replied with tremendous authority:

"Put that rat-bastard on the phone!"

"But Aunt Livia—"

"Cut the crap, you little tight-puss bitch!"

Candy summoned all her dignity. "I'm sorry, Aunt Livia," she said, "but I don't propose to be talked to like that by *anyone*. Furthermore, I simply don't know *what* you're talking about. Good-bye!"

With that she replaced the phone firmly in its cradle and stood up to brush off her bathrobe, for she'd been unconsciously crumbling the piece of toast she'd picked up and her lap now was completely covered with it. She was quite certain that she had done the 'right thing.' Really, there were limits to—to how much vulgarity one could permit and—

The phone rang again, cutting short this train of thought.

"Where do you suppose he is then?" Livia asked in a quite normal tone of voice, just as if the conversation had not been interrupted.

"I've no idea," Candy replied. "Have you tried phoning his office?"

"His office? No, I haven't tried that. That's not a bad idea. I'll do that right now. . . . I'll catch up with that rat-ass and believe me, when I *do* . . ." and she hung up.

Candy sat silently for a second, her eyes fixed on the telephone. She was waiting for it to ring again, and for that raucous, unladylike voice to complete its demolition of the lovely summer morning. As for the *Miraculous Mandarin Suite,* it had come to an end and the radio was now delivering an extremely nasal rendition of "The Wabash Cannonball."

Candy bit her full lower lip in annoyance, and had just

begun to pour herself a cup of espresso coffee when the bell rang again.

She placed the half-filled cup on the table with a little crash of exasperation and picked up the phone. There was no answer—and yet, the bell kept ringing. Then she realized that it was the front door; she had absurdly confused it with the phone.

Ordinarily she would have thought of such an error as no more than amusing; but not this morning. Coming after the stormy events of the past few days, this little stumble that her mind had made struck her as being significant—ominous as well. My nerves have had about as much as they can stand, she thought as she went to answer the door.

In the doorway stood a very thin old man dressed in a messenger boy's uniform.

"Telegram for Miss Christian," he said. He was blinking violently.

Candy noticed how slender and delicate his wrist was when she took the envelope. She looked at him again. He seemed to be on the verge of tears. "Is there anything wrong? I mean are you feeling ill, or—"

"Something in my eye," he explained.

"Something in your eye! Well, for goodness sake don't *rub* it like that!"

(He had taken out a handkerchief and was patting at his eye.)

Candy had to stoop down to look into his eye—he was quite short. As she did so her bathrobe opened considerably and, since this took place a few inches before his face, he found himself staring at her bare throat and splendid young breasts. . . .

"No, not that way," she ordered, "look up!"

"*Boy!*" he muttered enthusiastically, squinting as best he could with his watery and twitching eye at Candy's luscious chest.

Even if he *had* looked up it wouldn't have been much good—he was standing in the doorway with the light behind him and it was impossible to see the speck in his eye. Impulsively, the young girl took him by the lapels of his jacket and drew him into the room where she turned him this way and that trying to get the proper light.

After a few minutes of this she ended up sitting on a sofa with the elderly messenger boy stretched out beside her and his head in her lap.

He had yielded limply when she had bent him down backward and now, as she leaned over him, her left breast became almost entirely disengaged from the bathrobe and loomed above his face. He snapped at it weakly, missing it by a few inches.

While Candy's attention was wholly engaged in trying to remove the speck from his eye, the elderly messenger boy continued to regard her breast peevishly, and now and again lunged feebly, like a sick seal, at it. Finally, he paused, his mouth watering profusely as Candy stared at the red, winking eye. "I'll have it out in a jiffy!" she announced cheerfully, then ordered: "Hold still!" And, as she twisted to and fro, the flimsily attached bathrobe really opened and *both* her pert, inquisitive young breasts appeared. "Don't move!" she admonished. "I *think* I see it!"

The aged fellow held still as requested, but an instant

later, when Candy leaned forward abruptly, bringing her fantastic breasts to within an inch of his face, he lost all semblance of control and dived desperately into the open bathrobe.

Candy was so taken aback that she sat stock-still at first, and for a few seconds the thin old man rooted and wallowed between her breasts, rubbing them with his nose and muttering wildly to himself.

"Now *listen* . . ." she said, suddenly realizing what was up. "What in the *world* are you doing!" and she pushed him firmly from her lap.

He fell immediately to the floor and lay there on his back with his frail limbs waving slowly like a beetle's. Then he managed to stagger to his feet and shuffle to the open door. . . .

"Good-bye, darling," he gulped, pausing there and blinking rapidly four or five times.

Candy waited till she was sure he was gone before she crossed the room and shut the door. "*Well!*" she said to herself. "I wonder what the messenger-service people would think if they knew that one of their messengers—" She stopped, noticing the telegram which she'd all but forgotten in the confusion. She stooped and got it from the floor, opened it and read:

EXPECTING YOU HOSPITAL 10:30 A.M.
                                                DR. J. DUNLAP.

Good Grief, I'll barely have time to *dress*, she thought and shuddered slightly—a chill feeling of foreboding had come over her as she read the message, and she couldn't shake it off. . . .

By taking a taxi she managed to arrive at the Racine County Hospital at 10:30 on the dot. She hurried into the first door she saw, which didn't happen to be the main entrance, and found herself standing in a gleaming long corridor flanked by spotless white doors. She started walking tentatively, looking for an office of some kind where she could state her business. Each door seemed very much like the next and she finally opened one at random, and went in, hoping to find a nurse or someone who would be able to tell her where to find Dr. Dunlap.

She saw at once that she was in one of the sickrooms. There was a disheveled bed, and squatting on the floor for some reason was the occupant.

It was a woman in her seventies with very long gray hair and wearing a white nightgown.

"Git out!" she said in a cranky voice.

"Oh!" Candy said. "Oh—I'm so sorry," and she carefully shut the door.

After this she was more prudent, but when she came to a door with a bronze plaque on it on which was engraved *OSPHRESIOLAGNIA*, she paused. From inside she could hear the clicking of a typewriter. It stopped when she knocked and a deep masculine voice said: *"Come in."*

Seated behind a desk was a dark good-looking young man. His deep brown eyes were the most sensitive and the most intelligent that Candy felt she had ever seen, and his nose was thin, with a fine aristocratic curve.

Her heart gave a little jump in that first instant of their

meeting, and she even had time to think: Perhaps all the rest of my life I shall recall this moment—and then the silence was broken by his sonorous voice, as he cleared his throat and leaned forward slightly, placing his hands gracefully, almost protectingly, on the typewriter.

"Are you here for masturbation?" he inquired briskly.

"I beg your pardon?" said Candy. It was just possible, she thought, that she hadn't heard right.

The young man held his fist up and agitated it meaningfully, yet with such a disinterested air that his gesture—ordinarily such a smutty one—seemed quite abstract and inoffensive. "You know—onanism—'*beating your meat,*'" he explained.

"Oh no!" Candy declared, quite taken aback. "I'm not sure why I'm here . . . but it certainly couldn't be for *that!*"

"You said 'that' in a peculiar sort of way—as if you thought there were something wrong with the subject," observed the young man behind the desk, his eyes flashing belligerently.

"Well I—I said, er—I didn't mean to make a *value* judgment," she stammered, terribly flustered.

"I see," he said coldly.

"But isn't it unhealthy? I mean, masturbation *is* bad for the complexion, isn't it?"

The young man stared at her with scientific detachment and said nothing.

What she had just uttered sounded idiotic to her and she tried frantically to think of some way to repair the damage, but nothing came to mind. She stood, blushing crimson for an unbearable few seconds, then, unable to stand the tension any longer, she wheeled and bolted – dashing out the door so precipitously that she collided with a nurse who was coming down the hall.

The nurse—a small stocky brunette—stepped back, clenched her fist and prepared to punch Candy in the jaw. (You had to be ready for trouble every moment in a hospital; and anyone who came flying violently out of *that* door could quite easily be psychotic.)

Candy excused herself as best she could and asked the nurse where the administration office was.

"Well, it's not in *there,*" the nurse replied warily, indicating the room Candy had just rushed out of. (She still wasn't sure she might not be dealing with some kind of raving, anal-erotic maniac.)

"Yes," Candy said dryly, "I found that out. . . . But whose office *is* that? I mean there was a young man in there who . . ."

"Dr. Irving Krankeit," the nurse cut in.

"Dr. Irving Krankeit," Candy repeated musingly. "And he's—?"

"He's our staff psychiatrist."

"Oh, I see! I was just wondering because some of the things he said were—Well, I understand of course, if he's a psychiatrist . . ."

The nurse nodded sympathetically, then growing secretive, she suddenly grasped Candy's elbow and drew her several paces down the hall. "Dr. Krankeit's theories *are* unconventional," she confided in a low voice. "*Very* unconventional."

"Oh?"

The nurse grew even more conspiring. Her voice

threatening to descend to a whisper, she said: "Yes, *he* believes that the way to clear up our mental problems, and to settle all the troubles in the world is to get everyone to—" She broke off, regarding the young girl uncertainly.

"Yes?" said Candy, eager to learn.

". . . to—well, you've heard the title of his book, haven't you?"

"I'm afraid I haven't," said Candy.

"It's called . . . *Masturbation Now!*" the nurse said, forming each syllable slowly with her lips and making almost no sound. Then she sucked in her cheeks appraisingly.

"That certainly *is* an unconventional idea," Candy admitted.

"*He* claims that *normal* sex relations," the nurse went on, "cause all these mental disorders so many people have, and he says that *his* way would stop War!"

Candy thought of Dr. Krankeit's earnest young face, the evident sincerity of his dark beseeching eyes. . . . Surely he was honest! . . . and dedicated too, and—and sweet and kind. . . . "Well," she said philosophically, "maybe the world *needs* some shocking new notion like that to make men stop fighting with each other."

"Your guess is as good as mine," the squat little nurse said shrugging, and with that she turned on her heel and started to walk away. " 'Reception' is down that way," she called back, "turn right at the end of the corridor," and she pointed to the way from which she herself had come.

Candy followed these instructions and soon found herself in a waiting room for visitors and "out-patients."

The several people sitting about all put down their magazines and ceased their whispered conversations to stare at the newcomer; and Candy, feeling quite self-conscious, went straight to the reception desk and presented to the woman there the telegram she'd received. The receptionist was a small, birdlike woman whose name, according to a sign on the desk, was Mrs. Prippet.

"Have a seat," she said, having scarcely glanced at the telegram and regarding Candy fixedly as if there were something extremely curious about the lovely young girl standing before her.

Candy hesitated. "This came this morning," she said, indicating the telegram. She paused, and Mrs. Prippet and the people seated about looked at her expectantly. "I wonder if you could tell me . . ." her voice trailed off uncertainly—everyone in the room was listening with great interest and she was especially intimidated by the receptionist, Mrs. Prippet, who was looking at her with a pained expression as if Candy were speaking some sort of grotesquely broken English.

"You *are* Candy Christian?"

"Why yes, I—"

"Then *please* sit down," Mrs. Prippet said icily. "Dr. Dunlap will see you as soon as he's free."

Candy turned only to face a barrage of silent eyes. Not until she had found a seat did they leave off and, with a rustle of pages and dry whispers, go back to their previous occupations. And now that she was safely ensconced, Candy, in turn, began to look at *them,* stealing furtive glimpses and turning quickly away whenever another pair of exploring eyes clashed with her own. . . .

Sitting opposite was a fat girl about her own age, and her throat was horribly distended with goiter. Candy looked at it for five seconds in fascination before realizing that she was "staring." She turned then, angry with herself. For heaven's sake, she thought, a thing like that is merely an accidental glandular condition; it has nothing whatsoever to do with what the girl's *really* like. She might be someone with a great awareness of Beauty . . . a sculptress perhaps, or a magnificent contralto . . . well no, not a contralto . . .

She continued taking inventory. There were two nuns; one old, one young, but both pale and wearing eyeglasses with silver rims. From time to time the younger one hissed something to her companion who would give no sign of having heard anything. Near them a young couple, the woman pregnant, whispered together. And finally, a man wearing Bermuda shorts and a sport jacket whose face she couldn't see since he was holding a copy of *National Geographic* in front of it. Candy's gaze lingered on the man's knees and calves, which were a bit plump she thought, and then she realized with a start that *he* was looking at *her*— peeping, that is, through the fingers that held the magazine, and, presumably, watching her reaction to his plump knees. . . .

She looked hastily away and her eyes were drawn to the goiter again; but this time its owner caught her in the act, and stared fiercely back at her. Candy didn't know *which* way to turn and was considering just shutting her eyes when a man with snow-white hair and a goatee strode into the waiting room.

There was a disinct elegance about this man, Candy thought, something chivalric—a natural grace in the way his body bent from the waist almost as if he were bowing.

Suddenly he straightened bolt upright and stared at *her,* at Candy! Then he bent down quickly again, whispered something. . . . Mrs. Prippet was eying her too now and was nodding "yes" with her head. . . .

"Miss Christian," she called.

Candy sprang up and came to the desk. Once again all eyes focused on her, and a warm blush welled up, darkening her pretty face. It was like being the point of interest in a stadium, she thought, as she gracefully took her position before the man with the snowy hair.

Mrs. Prippet cleared her throat, and said, in a whisper everyone in the room could hear, "Dr. Dunlap would like to ask you a few questions, Miss Christian," and then added ominously, "Dr. Dunlap is the *Director* of our hospital."

Candy expected that the courtly gentleman would invite her to his office at this point, but such an idea didn't seem to occur to him. He was staring at her in an extraordinarily blunt fashion.

"Yes," he said in a rasping whisper, spacing each word slowly and distinctly, "I most certainly *would* like to ask Miss Christian 'a few questions!' "

Needless to say, his vehemence discomforted Candy still further.

There followed a pause now, during which the distinguished-looking doctor glared sternly at Candy as if to see whether she dared say anything. The suspense increased by the second; everyone in the waiting room leaned forward, hardly breathing, and shamelessly attentive. . . .

This would have been a good moment for Candy herself to suggest that they retire to Dr. Dunlap's private office, but she discovered she was incapable of speaking. Helplessly she glanced about at the audience with their bulging eyes, then, mutely entreating, she turned again to the director. . . .

Either Dr. Dunlap didn't understand this plea, or else he simply didn't care. He held his hands clasped behind his back and stood with his feet spaced well apart, and now, just before he addressed her, he rose up and down on his toes several times in a terrifying imitation of Charles Laughton in *Mutiny on the Bounty*.

"*Miss Christian*," he snarled in an ear-splitting whisper, "your father was admitted to this hospital two nights ago with an extremely grave head injury, suffering from shock, loss of blood, and possible concussion. . . . He had been dealt a violent blow to the frontal lobe of his brain—a blow, which, if by some miracle does not prove fatal, will nevertheless probably leave him mentally impaired for the rest of his life!" Dr. Dunlap paused, carefully breathed three times, rising up and down on his toes as he did, then went on even more slowly and pompously than before. "Last night, Miss Christian, at a time when your father was hovering so closely to death that the slightest disturbance might have sealed his fate, one of our nurses, hearing a noise, entered the room and found you . . . *stark naked, writhing, wallowing* and—and—and—COPULATING ON THE FLOOR OF THAT SICKROOM!"

A gasp of triumph—almost of relief—burst from the crowd at this revelation. The girl with the goiter slapped herself on the thigh as if she had somehow guessed what was coming all along.

Dr. Dunlap had actually shouted the last few words of

his terrible accusation and now stood with his jowls trembling from the intensity of his emotions.

Mrs. Prippet, the receptionist, smiled proudly, and as for poor Candy, her knees suddenly sagged and she felt as though she were going to swoon.

"No," she moaned. "No . . . no . . ."

"*What!*" the director demanded indignantly. "I say that you were *seen*, you and some man, having wanton inter-course on the floor under your father's bed! *Seen*—do you hear me? Seen going at it like a pair of HOT WART HOGS!!!" (He had begun to shout again, carried away like a holy-roller preacher.) "HORSING ON THE FLOOR! HUMPING UNDER THE BED! GROUSING IN THE GOODIE!"

"No, no," Candy sobbed, "oh please . . . please, please. PLEASE! You don't understand . . ."

"DON'T UNDERSTAND?" roared the director.

"Don't *understand?*" echoed the girl with the goiter, who had suddenly gotten to her feet in the excitement.

"No!" Candy cried. "You don't! . . . It isn't what you think!"

"Why the nerve of her!" the pregnant woman ex-claimed.

"She could have killed her own father—doing a thing like that right there under his nose," interjected the man in the Bermuda shorts.

"I'll have you know that this is a hospital, and not a . . . *house of ill-repute!*" Dr. Dunlap proclaimed.

"This is no place for a common young harlot to—"

"Oh!" Candy whimpered, flinching at every word.

"Another thing," volunteered the younger nun, "how

did her father *get* hurt? Who was it that struck him down . . . and *why?*"

Mrs. Prippet nodded her head vigorously in agreement and said:

"That's right! We haven't heard about *that* part yet."

"Probably did it herself," the young husband muttered.

"*Or* had her *boyfriend* do it," added his wife, giving him a dark look.

"I say that nobody in their right mind would come into their own father's sickroom and—and," said Dr. Dunlap, trying to develop his theory calmly and with scientific objectivity, but as he started to grope for words he lost control and was soon bellowing again: "TROLLOP! SLUT! FLOOSIE!"

"Could you sit down, please?" the young nun said to the girl with the goiter. "She can't see," she explained, indicating the old nun who was straining forward in her chair and trying to look around the others, but who was evidently too weak to stand up.

The plump girl did not sit down, but rather stepped to the side, considerately looking back to ascertain that she no longer obstructed the view.

For Candy, overwhelmed with embarrassment, it happened with the economy and the faultless logic of a dream: the girl stepping aside and looking back . . . moving her slablike arm out of the way . . . and finally, the toothless old nun revealed, leaning forward with visible relish to drink in what she'd been missing. . . .

"Good Grief!" Candy said aloud. "This is worse than a nightmare!"

Then she fainted.

seven

7

As Candy fell, a dark-haired young man who had been standing in the doorway entered the room and hurried to her side. It was Dr. Krankeit, who, hearing the sound of raised and angry voices, had stepped out of his office and come to the waiting room to investigate.

He had just time to understand that the girl, object and brunt of Dr. Dunlap's awful accusations, was the daughter of the recently admitted Mr. Christian—one of his patients—and then Candy slumped to the floor. . . .

In a moment he was on his knees next to her, taking her pulse and making sure that this collapse was not of a grave nature. Then, still kneeling, he raised his head and regarded Dr. Dunlap thoughtfully.

Ordinarily, Krankeit had such consummate control of his feelings that he often appeared to his patients and colleagues as emotionless; but now there was an angry glint in his expressive brown eyes when he addressed the director:

87

"Really, J. D., this is . . ." he paused, shaking his head incredulously as he sought to encompass the magnitude of it all, ". . . I mean were you *trying* to get this girl to faint? It's—it's simply *astonishing!*"

Suddenly Mrs. Prippet hurried from her desk and knelt beside him. "Here, dear," she said to Candy, whose eyes were fluttering open, "breathe in deeply—this will bring you round in a jiffy," and she held a small bottle under Candy's nose. Candy inhaled obediently several times before her eyes closed once more and her head slumped limply against Krankeit's shoulder. He regarded her for a moment, then snatched the flask from Mrs. Prippet and whiffed the contents.

"This isn't smelling-salts, you imbecile," he hissed, thrusting the bottle at her, "it's *ether!*"

Dr. Dunlap was quite silent now—as were all the others in the room—and visibly taken aback by what had occurred. It was not so much concern for Candy's welfare that distressed him as it was his embarrassment before the onlookers—the incident had taken an unfortunate turn and was clearly showing an aptitude for becoming a small scandal. Worst of all, Krankeit had witnessed the thing, and might utilize it to undermine his (Dunlap's) position at the hospital.

"You're quite right, Krankeit," he muttered suddenly, "I completely lost my head and behaved like an idiot— here, give me a hand. Let's get her into my office. She can lie on the couch till she comes around."

"No. Let's take her to my office. There are some questions I'd like to ask her," Krankeit said.

"Questions?" Dr. Dunlap's eyes widened and his jaw stiffened.

"About her father," explained Krankeit. "And I'd like to have her come with me when I examine him. That is," he added sarcastically, "if she's in any condition to do so."

Dr. Dunlap acquiesced. The sooner this whole affair could be transported behind a closed door the better. He took Candy under the arms and Krankeit took her legs and together they lifted her. At a frown from Dr. Krankeit, Dr. Dunlap shifted his grip—he had clasped his hands over Candy's shapely breasts—and held her by the armpits, which was much more awkward. Then they carried her off.

When they had laid her on the couch in Krankeit's office, Dunlap straightened up and stood morosely silent, not sure what to do next.

Arranging Candy's skirt, which had climbed high on her thighs, Krankeit said: "Perhaps it would be wiser if Miss Christian didn't see you first thing when she regains consciousness"—he paused, and suddenly his eyes flicked into Dr. Dunlap's watery gaze—"she might blow her stack," he said, and blew out a faint jet of well-inhaled cigarette smoke.

Dr. Dunlap slumped as if he'd been dealt a stiff body punch.

"Right," he said nodding limply, "but . . . but, Krankeit . . . there's something I'd like to ask . . . I mean about what happened here just now, I, eh . . . I trust you're not . . . I mean I realize the thing must have looked shocking to you, but it's a closed issue now and I hope—"

"Don't sob!" Krankeit snapped with contempt.

"*Don't sob?*" exclaimed the older man, his voice cracking, and, as if Krankeit's admonition were a signal, he
immediately began to sniff and wring his hands like a
little girl. "It's all very well for you to sit there and tell me
this and tell me that and tell me to get out and tell me not
to sob . . . You're a young man, your career's just beginning now and you haven't got a care in the world. You're
not sixty-one years old. *You* haven't been connected with
this hospital for twenty-two years! *You* don't have dis-
missal staring you in the face," he blubbered, "and with
just a few more months to go before retirement. . . ."

Eyes bulging, and gasping for breath, he paused. Then,
with a horrible contortion of his mouth which was meant
to be a smile, he said: "You know, Krankeit, I'm not such
a bad sort of guy—oh, I know we don't always see eye to
eye about everything—the latest techniques, the way the
hospital should be run. I know you must think I'm con-
servative, not up-to-date; perhaps a—a—"

"—a senile horse's ass?" Dr. Krankeit suggested callously.

Dr. Dunlap winced, and his pendulous lips quivered. It
seemed for a moment as if he might lose his head completely and begin squealing like an insane ape, but suddenly he regained his composure, and when he spoke
again he did so softly and not without dignity.

"You may not believe this," he said, "but I was very
much like you are now—when I was a young man. Hot-
headed . . . outspoken . . . I was pretty impatient with
the older men too, and I didn't give two hoots if they
heard me saying so either. Just the way you are. I suppose
that explains why—even though we've occasionally been
at loggerheads since you've come here—I, er—er—well, that

secretly, I liked you all the time. Sometimes, as a matter of fact, I almost feel as if I might be your *Dad.*" (Dr. Dunlap became a bit choked up again as he made this surprising revelation.) "Mrs. Dunlap and I don't have any children," he confessed, "but if we did have a son, I think I'd want him to be something like you. I don't know why I should be telling you all this; especially after everything that's been—" He stopped speaking brusquely and gaped at Candy.

The precious girl lay on her back moaning faintly, like some sleeper beset by an ugly dream. In her new position, though she was still unconscious, she had drawn her legs up, and, once again, the pleated black skirt had slipped up her legs, affording a breath-taking view of her marvelous bare limbs and the milk-white *V* the panties made, concealing her honeypot from the prying eyes of Dr. Dunlap— for that was exactly where his stare was focused.

When Krankeit noticed this he leaned over and arranged the skirt properly. He moved expertly and with assurance, as if these exposed legs belonged to *him.*

"Now, now," he said, returning his attention to Dunlap, "try to be a good boy. As you say, you've got just a few more months to go before retirement."

Dunlap blanched at this latest thrust, and his lips fairly jangled with distress. He said nothing though, and, after a moment, there came into his eyes a saintly look of sadness.

Something about this expression intrigued Krankeit very much. He recognized it, yet couldn't think of what it reminded him.

Great Scott! he thought suddenly. It was true! Dunlap actually *was* behaving as if he were his father!

There was no mistaking it—that look of patient suffering—he had seen it before on the face of his own
father. And now thinking about his father (who had disappeared when Krankeit was still a boy) he felt a jab of
remorse.

"Do you think it's nice," Dunlap sniffled, "to have your
every action pounced on by somebody and wrenched asun-
der?"

Krankeit crushed his cigarette out in an ashtray and
said:

"It's not *you,* it's the damned shell you're imprisoned in
that I'm trying to jack off—er, I mean *wrench* off."

"What do you mean by that?" Dunlap asked in a hurt
tone.

"Just this: you've an ocean of drowned impulses to *jack
off!* All your life something's been preventing you—first
your mother, then you yourself. You come from the last
'primitive' generation before Freud discovered copulation;
you have a veneer of high moral virtue, but deep down
you're a veritable sewer of bestiality and lust!"

This analysis of his character seemed to please Dr. Dunlap more than anything else, and he perked up a bit.
Krankeit was, at least, taking a serious interest in him as a
personality, which was a clear improvement over his
former, uniformly vitriolic attitude.

"I'm taking advantage of the fact that you symbolically
adopted me as your son a little while ago, to speak frankly
—in 'family intimacy'—to you about this thing," Krankeit
said.

At the words "adopted me as your son," and again, at
the words "family intimacy," Dunlap's eyes welled with

happiness, and his spine began to straighten in sturdy little jerks—*Exactly like an erection!* thought Krankeit, taking a step forward, his hands cupped and raised as a ready catalyst for the process, before he checked himself.

"You know, my boy," said Dunlap, "there's a great deal of good sense in what you've said about me. I *have* been holding myself in all my life. As you say, I was brought up to look on sex as an evil and forbidden subject, and I suppose that's why I've always been fascinated by its symbols—the body of this young woman, for instance. But how about you?"

"What about me?"

"Well, how do *you* feel when you look at her—you who are from a younger generation, and who have made a deliberate effort to rid yourself of old-fashioned notions?"

Krankeit looked at Candy blankly.

"She'd look like Marilyn Monroe in that calendar picture," Dr. Dunlap pointed out, "if she didn't have any clothes on."

"If you'd read my book, you'd understand how I feel about these things," Krankeit said. "In the fifth chapter of *Masturbation Now!* I state expressly that heterosexual love-making is the root of all neuroses, a shabby illusion which misleads the ego, that we must endeavor to keep it in its true place—as an aid, and adjunct to masturbation, which is the only sex-mode that permits complete fulfillment and mental health."

Dr. Dunlap listened with utmost seriousness. "It certainly was a courageous book," he said, looking at Krankeit with paternal admiration. "In it you defy all the conventional sex mores."

Krankeit smiled complacently and said: "Of course, for someone like you, who hasn't got *any* sex-orientation, heterosexuality is the logical starting place—it's certainly better than nothing. Theoretically, there's nothing wrong at all with that impulse you have to look at this girl's body—it's even a very good thing that you've finally gotten up nerve to do it."

Nervily, Dunlap turned and looked at Candy as she lay stretched out on her side on the couch. Just then she sighed, and rolled on her back as before. Her sweet knees lifted and her skirt slid back so that the white frilled *V* of her panties showed again. The righteousness quickly drained from Dunlap's eyes and was replaced by a hard, corrupted glint.

"Of course," Krankeit went on, "for myself, I've never had much time for those things—too busy with my work."

Dunlap said nothing. He was keeping his eyes trained on the scalloped *V*, beneath which pulsed Candy's precious little lamb-pit.

"Yes, first there was med school, and then my research and writing . . . I've had little time for anything else . . . no romance, no family life . . . I've missed that though—the family life."

"Is that so?" said Dunlap, who had been paying no attention whatever and hadn't the least idea what had just been said.

"Yes, it is. When you spoke about feeling like my Dad a little while ago, I couldn't help being a bit touched. You see—I never knew my own father." A slight huskiness came into Krankeit's voice as he said this.

Dunlap said nothing. He was stooping over slightly in Candy's direction and staring at her intently.

"To get back to what I was saying," continued Krankeit, "you're terribly jammed up. This mechanism you've contrived to keep your sexual lust a secret from the world, and from you yourself, is causing you more trouble than you realize. That's why I decided it was all right for you to look at Miss Christian's legs—it's exactly what you need."

"Exactly what I need," echoed Dr. Dunlap like a zombie, and moved a few inches closer to the luscious form on the couch with his fingertips twitching spasmodically.

"It's a thousand times better for you to satisfy that sort of desire, than to fight it down and have it haunt your Unconscious for years to come," said Krankeit persuasively.

"Dunlap . . . I say, DUNLAP!!"

Dr. Dunlap had quickly stepped to Candy and he was wrestling off her panties in a veritable frenzy. "I thought you said it was 'exactly what I needed,' " he mumbled, confounded now.

"Ah yes, but only up to the point where it doesn't interfere with some *other* party. That's an important distinction."

Dr. Dunlap finished pulling Candy's panties over her shoes and flung them over his shoulder, where they settled like a silken butterfly on Krankeit's typewriter. Candy was now delightfully nude from the waist down and lying on her back. Unhesitatingly, the hospital director put his hands on her legs and drew them apart . . .

"DUNLAP!!"

Dr. Dunlap hastily placed his hand on the pulsing jelly-box he'd exposed, with the air of a little boy caught doing wrong, and wishing to hide the evidence. "All right," he said peevishly, after a moment during which Krankeit merely glared at him, "I'll put them back on."

By "them," he obviously meant Candy's panties, yet he made no step to retrieve them. He stood, his knees slightly bent, forthrightly facing Krankeit; and his hand resting politely on Candy's golden *V*.

Krankeit's expressive brown eyes flashed impatiently. *"Well, what are you waiting for?"* he said.

"All right, all right," exclaimed Dunlap, "how many times do you want me to say it?"

Dr. Dunlap behaved as if there were nothing in the situation of an emergency nature—certainly nothing for Krankeit to lose his head over and raise his voice. . . .

"DUNLAP!!!"

(Krankeit had just noticed that Dr. Dunlap appeared to have only four fingers on the hand in question—that his little finger had treacherously sneaked *into* the orifice.)

"Look here, Krankeit, there's no need to shout," Dr. Dunlap said, "we're not in the ghetto you know."

Dr. Krankeit pretended to ignore this racial allusion, but when he next spoke the volume of his voice had lessened considerably and was rife with Princetonian modulations. Nevertheless it was very firm.

"If you don't take your finger out of Miss Christian this very instant, and replace her undergarment, I shall report what you're doing *in detail* to the board of trustees."

This turned the trick; Dunlap let go and went to retrieve the precious little garment, wagging his hand incredulously the while to an imaginary—and sympathetic—

onlooker in the corner. "Krankeit, the great rebel, the man who had the guts to *jack off* in the face of a Supreme Court decision, is shocked," he said. He slipped the panties over Candy's shoes and pulled them up into place. This was a bit complicated—he wasn't in the habit of putting underwear on young girls—and, of course, his hand got caught inside and remained there.

"Good Lord!" said Krankeit, exasperated. "If you're going to poke your finger into that girl every three minutes you could at least put a p.c. on." (p.c., standing for pinky cheater, was hospital slang for the rubber fingers gynecologists wear during digital examinations.)

Dunlap fumbled ineptly for a little while before finally freeing his trapped hand.

"After all," he said, looking abused, "I was only following your advice—trying not to suppress something and have it haunt my Unconscious."

"It gets a little more complicated when you begin to involve another party. I didn't say that you could just walk up to a strange woman in the street and interfere with her genitals, you know."

"But that's just it!" Dunlap exclaimed. "This one is unconscious; she doesn't know what's happening . . . and, since it does me such a lot of good and doesn't affect her in the slightest, why shouldn't—"

"Just what do you want to *do?*" Krankeit asked, narrowing his eyes.

Dr. Dunlap fingered his goatee in meditation. "Let's examine her," he said brightly.

Krankeit, with revulsion, pictured the two of them poring over the naked girl like a couple of scholars with a rare manuscript.

"What the hell, she's only a shicker," Dunlap said with a conniving wink.

"Only a *what?*"

"A shicksy? I'm not sure I'm pronouncing it right—it's Jewish, means a Gentile girl . . ."

"I wouldn't know," said Krankeit coldly.

Dunlap's vernacularism—intended to invoke a hot gush of friendship—had the contrary result. And there had been that remark about the ghetto, Krankeit thought. Dunlap was beginning to harp on the subject.

Subject was hardly the word to describe Krankeit's feelings about his Jewmanship—a muscle with the outer skin flayed off, twitching violently in the air, gives a more accurate idea. For someone to say something to him—as Dunlap had just done—which referred in any way to Jewishness, was like poking a finger in his eye.

This time it had come in mirthful form, which was the most familiar pattern—the Gentile, in a mood of alcoholic joviality, shows off the Jewish term (usually vulgar) which he has learned. To his mind, this ought to please and flatter the Jew, witnessing as it does his knowledge and appreciation of the latter's culture. Instead, the Jew—jumpy as an eyeball—feels such a remark is patronizing and disrespectful.

At any rate, that was how Krankeit himself reacted. The idea, so touching in itself, of Dunlap's spiritual paternity was summarily dismissed from his mind. The director became like some unknown figure passed in the street—a stranger, and therefore, an enemy.

Krankeit retreated into the depths of the room and sat behind his desk. Fussing with a packet of papers, he said: "I wonder if you could drop back this afternoon, Doctor. I've got some work here I'd like to wrench off."

He kept his eyes fixed on the surface of his desk all the time that Dunlap stood hesitating and clearing his throat . . . and for several minutes after the door had clicked shut. Then he got up, moving like a serpent, and quickly crossed the room.

eight

8

Candy was coming to. Before her eyes reality swirled effulgently, then resolved itself into a sharp, pricking sensation in her backside. She was half lying, half standing against some sort of board or table, and her wrists were attached to it. She couldn't see very well what was going on behind her, but in the next instant she felt again as if someone were sticking a pin into her buttocks.

"Hey!" she said. "Stop that!"

"Ah," said a rich masculine voice behind her. "Good . . . it worked!"

Straining her neck, she turned and found herself staring into the tragic brown eyes of the young man into whose office she had stumbled earlier that afternoon.

"I was just using a bit of acupuncture, the ancient Chinese pin-therapy, to see if I couldn't bring you back to consciousness," he said. "Now just hold still while I take them out."

Candy looked over her shoulder and was startled to see a number of silver pins projecting from her marvelously round derriere. Surpisingly, she hardly felt them, but a dark blush colored her face at the idea that this young man, sitting inches behind her, was extracting pins from her bare bottom.

". . . you were out for quite a while," he was saying, chatting calmly, ". . . partly an accident . . . someone gave you ether to inhale by mistake . . . so I decided to try the pins. . . . I wasn't sure I was getting the 'points' correctly."

" 'Points?' " Candy said. She was still quite dazed and couldn't think what had led up to this incredible awakening.

"Oh yes! It wouldn't do to stick them in any old place, you know. There are important neural points in the body —418 in all—and by placing the pins in certain combinations of the points it's possible to speed up, or slow down, the functioning of the various internal organs."

Candy wondered whether *all* the points were located in such incongruous areas, but she said nothing, being much too absorbed in a rapid inspection of the room to locate her skirt and panties.

Krankeit had detached her hands from the metal rings that held them—she had been on some sort of tilted operating table—and now, as she crossed the room to retrieve her clothes, she suppressed an impulse to cover her adorable pubes. But, she thought, after all he *was* a doctor, and accustomed to seeing naked women—mightn't it look terribly *bête* for her to try and hide herself like that?

"Was I unconscious for very long?" she asked, trying to sound calm and assured.

"For about a half hour. But are you feeling all right now? Because I'd like you to assist me. I'm about to examine your father, and your presence could be very helpful. He hasn't been able to recall his identity yet and, when he sees you, perhaps it will aid him to overcome his amnesia."

"Do you—do you think my father's mind has been permanently impaired?" Candy asked, half afraid to hear what the answer would be.

"It's hard to say. I don't know yet which of his mental faculties have been affected, or how severely. That's the purpose of this examination. We'll do our very best, of course, but only time will reveal the full extent of his injury. But are you sure you're feeling well enough to assist at the examination? It may be upsetting, you know."

"Yes, I know," said Candy, slipping into her panties and skirt—and she very nearly added that she was already feeling much better, simply from being dressed again, but she could see that such matters were of no concern to him. There was a moment of silence during which she looked deeply into Krankeit's troubled brown eyes, and thought crossly to herself, Good heavens, it's *Daddy's* condition we're concerned with—not *mine!*

And making a final adjustment to her sweet little blouse, Candy spoke decisively: "I'm ready, Dr. Krankeit."

nine

9

Lengthening her pace to accord with his, Candy stole a glance at Krankeit as he strode determinedly through the white halls, bent slightly forward, and with his hawklike nose cleaving the air before him like the cone of a medium-range guided missile.

She wondered, couldn't this striding along together of theirs be a symbol of all that was to come? In the bright triumphs of his medical career, and also in the moments of anguish and doubt when it seemed to him that all his efforts were to end in ignominious failure—she would be at his side, marching along, as at present, to the next encounter with the Enemy, and lending him the soft assuring warmth of her femininity.

Candy Krankeit, she thought with a bittersweet thrill—so that was how it was to be! All those dreamy-girl hours spent wondering whom her fate would bring . . . what the forceful male presence would be like that would pro-

vide her with the key to fling open the gates of her woman-
hood—and then, on a day like the others, she opened a
door and there was the man that put an end to all her
games of reverie. As simple as that.

And this meant that *she,* in turn, must be the instrument
of *his* release, though he hadn't as yet sensed it of course.
This fact, that Krankeit was still unaware of their looming,
destined love, only endeared him to her the more. The
poor darling ninny, she thought, little did he realize the
stark, aching need he had for her. She almost laughed
aloud thinking of this obtuseness of his—so like a man too.
There he was, all wrapped up in thoughts of his work,
never dreaming what his heart held in store for him. She
felt like pinching him, or playfully giving him a push, just
to break through his absurd masculine numbness; but it
was too soon, she knew, and it wouldn't do to disconcert
him just now when he needed all his calmness and lucidity
for the examination of her father.

Poor Daddy, she thought, and it's all my fault too! Well,
I'll make it up to him somehow. I'll—

Just then Krankeit turned sharply and entered a short,
vaulted hallway, and Candy's speculations were broken off
as sharply by what she saw there. . . .

The hall they were in terminated in a flight of stairs leading down, and, halfway to the stairs, was a middle-aged,
brick-shaped woman lying on her stomach on the floor.

Hearing Candy and Krankeit approaching, she raised
herself heavily to her knees and began to scrub the floor
with a wet and soapy brush. Evidently she had been taking
a break from her work when they had entered the hall.
Then, as they got closer, the woman looked up at Candy

with an expression of such fierce hostility that the girl almost stopped in her tracks. But Krankeit kept on walking and even said, "Good afternoon, Audrey," to the scrubwoman, who lowered her head, as if refusing to answer or even look at them, and muttered angrily under her breath as they passed. She did not stop her scrubbing to let them by and Candy actually had to step over her arm. But, a second after they had passed, the thickset woman impulsively tipped a bucket of soapy water she was using, and sent a good-size puddle of it flowing swiftly under Candy's high heels . . .

Candy was looking at Krankeit at that moment, trying to determine what his reaction was to this disagreeable person. She had just the time to see that he seemed completely oblivious—and then the treacherous liquid reached her feet and she began to slip. She realized with horror that she was in danger of tumbling down the flight of stairs, which was very close now, and, in that instant, the silence of the hospital corridor was shattered by a bloodcurdling roar of laughter!

Startled from his bemusement, Krankeit finally saw what was happening and managed to grab Candy's arm just as she was about to launch into space; then, having steadied her, he glanced back with a long look of revulsion at "Audrey," the scrubwoman, who was making no attempt to conceal her joy at the near-accident, or to still the laughter that echoed so diabolically in the hall.

"Gosh!" said Candy, when they had descended the stairs and were out of earshot of the husky scrubwoman. "Who was *that?*"

"Hmm?" Krankeit seemed to have already forgotten the incident.

"That woman—the woman who was washing the floor. Who *was* she?"

"Who was she? Why, she was a woman washing the floor." He said this in the soothing manner of a psycho-analyst addressing a nervous patient.

"Yes, but you called her 'Audrey.' "

"Well, why shouldn't I have? It's her name, you see," said Krankeit a bit brusquely.

"That's what I mean. You seemed to *know* her . . . know about her, that is. She seemed so strange, so—"

"I fail to see anything remarkable about her, or about the fact that I know her name: I happen to know the names of many people who work in the hospital."

He seemed to be getting a little angry and Candy diplomatically dropped the subject. Cranky old darling, she thought, but it was easy to see how the enormous strain of his work had gotten him on edge.

Uncle Jack, his head and a good bit of his face swathed in bandages, sat propped against pillows like an Oriental pasha and regarded his young visitors with a gentle smile.

"I've brought Candy to visit you," the young man had said.

"Candy? I knew a girl named Candy," Uncle Jack reminisced. "Looked just like this girl too . . . Could be her twin sister."

Just before coming in, Krankeit had explained the patient's condition to Candy, pointing out that he had become a more or less "disembodied intelligence," and could be expected to lack the most elementary knowledge about himself or even the ordinary details of existence. His *id* and his *ego*—both so central to rational conduct—had suffered near obliteration; and consequently, though he might be quite conscious of what was going on about him, it was like the awareness of a camera or a microphone, for he had practically no feeling of self.

Despite this briefing, Candy couldn't restrain a sigh of distress when Uncle Jack told her she reminded him of herself.

"But Daddy," she said, fighting hard to keep her voice steady, "it's *me,* it's Candy!"

Apparently Uncle Jack didn't feel this statement was intended for him, for he looked at Krankeit smilingly as if expecting *him* to answer.

Krankeit had taken out pad and pencil, and now jotted down the words *"agonic id."* He too was smiling, but in a different way than the patient. He was happy because this was his work, his element; he was like an expert operator seated before some fantastically complex switchboard, and he was about to determine which of its circuits were clear and which had been interrupted. Silently, he took Uncle Jack's hand and placed it, fingers spread apart, on the blanket. "Where is your thumb?" he asked.

Uncle Jack's angelic smile slowly froze on his face.

"Which one of your fingers is your thumb?" the young doctor repeated patiently.

Uncle Jack looked at his hand, perplexed. After a while, the middle finger raised up.

"Which is the middle finger then?"

This time the little finger lifted hesitantly.

"Ring finger?"

Nothing happened.

"Little finger?"

Uncle Jack's middle finger bobbed up again.

Krankeit reached over and lifted Uncle Jack's thumb. "What's that?" he inquired.

Uncle Jack smiled with relief. "You knew it all the time," he said admiringly.

Krankeit took hold of the little finger and held it up. "Which is that?"

"*Pinky!*" the patient said delightedly. "I'm pretty sure, pretty sure of that."

Candy was barely able to suppress a sob at this. Oh, poor dear Daddy, she thought, and it's all my fault, every last bit of it. . . .

"Which is your right hand?" Krankeit said, continuing his examination.

"I'll have to guess on that one. I get all mixed up," Uncle Jack explained, presenting his left hand.

"Which is your left hand?"

Uncle Jack looked intently at his hand, but said nothing.

"Which is your left foot?"

He presented his left little finger.

"Are you sure that's your left *foot?*"

He offered his right little finger.

"Which is your right thumb?"

"I'm all mixed up," said Uncle Jack, pointing to his left hand, then to his right hand, then to Krankeit's left foot. "I'm kind of mixed up on them," he confessed. "I never could get them straight."

Krankeit now took a number of heterogeneous objects from his pockets, humming cheerfully the while, and placed them on the patient's night table. Then he pointed to each one and carefully named it.

Uncle Jack's attention was apparently focused on this procedure: however, when asked to pick up the matches he picked up a pencil; asked to pick up the lighter he picked up a penknife; asked to pick up the chewing gum he did so and hurriedly chewed it; asked to pick up the pencil he picked up the gum again. . . .

"Is my arm up or down?" asked Krankeit, holding his left hand up and jotting busily on his pad with his right hand.

"I believe it's . . . *up;* not too positive though."

"Where is the ceiling?"

Uncle Jack looked up at the ceiling.

"Is it up?" Krankeit prompted.

"I'm gonna say up."

"Where is the floor?"

"It's down there."

"Is it up or down?"

Uncle Jack was silent for a few seconds, and then he said, "I'm gonna give up."

Krankeit pursed his lips reflectively as he framed the proper reply to bring the patient back into a more responsive syndrome, but before he could speak, the door sprang open and a chubby little man, followed by two women, entered the room.

Candy stood up from her chair in astonishment—it was Aunt Ida and her husband Luther, and with them, gaily waving a bunch of tulips, was Livia herself!

"Greetings, Gates!" Livia screamed merrily, laying the flowers on Uncle Jack's chest and friskily pinching his cheek. "We've come to cheer up our little sick boy!"

Ida and Luther, obviously wishing to disassociate themselves from this riotous entrance, hung back decorously at first, then stepped forward.

"Everything all right, Sidney?" asked Luther. "Not too bad?"

Aunt Ida, pale and gaunt, and grimly dressed in black, stared silently at her brother, her eyes glistening lugubriously.

Uncle Jack smiled sweetly in greeting. Not a bit of resistance from *him* if people wanted to call him "Sidney" or "Daddy," or anything else. And since in their minds he *was* "Sidney" and "Daddy," and since the real Sidney Christian was in a lost state similar to his own and in no condition to dispute the title, "Uncle Jack" *became* "Sidney" and "Daddy," and that was the end of it.

Livia had turned to wave hello to Candy, and now, for the first time, noticed the silent Krankeit. "Ah!" she said. "Dr. Livingstone, I presume."

A dark flush of annoyance clouded Krankeit's features. Ignoring Livia's brashness, he glanced quickly at his watch. "I have a consultation now," he informed Candy in a low voice. "I'll try and stop back here when I'm finished." Then, with a last look at Uncle Jack, he murmured, "Pity . . . We didn't even get to sounds and colors."

"Who's that Hebe doctor?" Livia said loudly before Krankeit was well out the door.

"Good Grief, Aunt Livia!" Candy flared. "Can't you ever . . . keep *still?*"

"Keep still?" Livia asked in genuine puzzlement.

"Candy's right," said Luther. "That was a tactless remark, and he couldn't possibly not have heard it. Couldn't you have waited till he was out of the room?"

"Oh my God!" Livia snorted in exasperation. "You've got to watch every damn little word with you people. Do you think that's going to help cheer up Sid, if we all sit around like that mopey Hebe doctor and don't say anything?"

Aunt Ida, who was arranging the tulips in a vase, sighed and exchanged looks of patient resignation with Candy and her husband—since Jack's disappearance, Livia had become worse than ever. . . .

"Poor old Sid," Livia went on. "Nothing to do but lie in bed and look at the four walls. He must be bored stiff." She was fumbling with a Pan American Airways satchel which she'd brought. "Well, we'll see if we can't cheer him up a little bit."

The others looked on in disapproval at the telltale sound of bottles clinking together in the satchel, but Uncle Jack, who had been supine in his bed, sat up with interest. "I could *do* with a drop of bourbon," he observed earnestly.

"Not bourbon, old boy," Livia corrected, extracting two bottles from her satchel and winking lewdly, "Schnapps! Steinhagen from the Tyrol! It'll juice you to the gills!"

"Now Livia, that's a darn silly idea to have brought that here," said Luther, puffing anxiously.

"Nonsense!" Livia snapped. "Just the thing for a hangover. Matter of fact, we could *all* probably stand a quick one. How about it, Ida? Neat or on the rocks? How about it, Can? Think you can scare up some ice cubes in this mausoleum?"

Candy was so angry she could have wept. "This—this is *incredible*," she said with a tiny stamp of rage.

"Oh really!" said Uncle Jack, sounding very lucid and urbane. "I don't see how a quick one could possibly do me any harm." He accompanied this remark with a look of calm severity—not to be gainsaid—in Candy's direction.

Aunt Livia had brought glasses too, and now set about improvising a bar on a large hospital wheeling-table. "There's a good girl, Can," she urged. "Ice cubes! And with all due dispatch! Remember, there's a brave little sick boy waiting for you to get back with the serum. So hurry! Mush! Mush!"

Candy flounced out of the room and cracked the door shut behind her.

Scarcely knowing where she was going or what she was going to do, she wandered blindly through the immaculate hospital halls. . . . In her mind, of course, was the desire to find Krankeit, but she soon became lost in the labyrinthine passages and stairways, and had no idea where to seek him.

Rounding a corner she faced yet another long corridor. Had she already traversed it? It was identical with the others and she felt the confused beginning sting of tears in her eyes as she started down it. Abruptly, a door on her left opened; a massive red arm reached out, seized her, and drew her into the room. . . .

She was in a kind of dimly lit, oversized closet full of brooms, mops and pails. . . . She stood there, petrified with fright, hardly daring to look at the person who had pulled her so fiercely into this sinister place.

Audrey, the squat, evil-tempered scrubwoman, leaned back against the door and eyed Candy impassively.

"You should excuse me," she said suddenly, "from yenking your arm so brutal."

Candy's arm *did* hurt, and she rubbed the spot ruefully, but she was vastly relieved that the terrifying little woman was merely *talking* to her—she had feared, at first, that her very life might be in danger.

"I wanted to have a chat with you," Audrey disclosed.

"Certainly," Candy agreed nervously.

"Just this: LEAVE MINE BOY ALONE!"

"Leave who? I'm afraid I don't—"

"Please!" cut in the stumpy scrubwoman. "I saw you with mine *Irving!* Lookin' at him—"

Candy regarded the powerful gray-haired woman with astonishment.

"—like salami wouldn't melt in your mouth!"

"Irving is your—your 'boy'?"

"Leave him alone! LEAVE MINE BOY ALONE!"

"Do—do you mean that you are Mrs. Krankeit—Dr. Krankeit's *mother?*"

"Yes. I am Irving's mother, but Mrs. Krankeit I am not. 'Krankeit' is a name that Irving made up because he didn't like our real name."

"Made it up? But why, what is your real name?"

"Semite," the squat little woman gravely replied. "Mrs. Silvia Semite."

Candy understood. She could guess at the untold hell the name "Irving Semite" must have caused Krankeit as a lad in his student days. But good grief, what a person's name was wasn't the *important* thing! She would make him see that. She would show him, when the time came, that she would be proud to become "Candy Semite."

"Irving changed his name because he's so sensitive," the scrubwoman pointed out proudly.

"But I don't understand. Why are you—" Candy stopped, staring at Mrs. Semite's soiled workclothes in utter bewilderment.

"You mean this?" and Irving's mother waved contemptuously at the mops and pails.

"Well . . . yes."

"It's so that I can be here, close to mine boy."

"But . . . but . . ." Candy looked about hopelessly at the brooms and dripping brushes.

"Irving, my son, is a genius," Mrs. Semite reminded Candy. "I want to be near him, to *see* him—every day. In his office I can't stay, I know—it 'embarrasses' him, and to the patients it looks funny to have his mother always standing there. All right. I understand that."

"And so you've taken on this job in order—in order to be near your son?"

"Exzectly. And no one should know I'm his mother . . . but to you I tell it, because I want you should leave Irving alone. You're not a nize girl for him!"

Candy looked away self-consciously and steeled herself for what was coming. No doubt Irving's mother had also heard the story about her and was going to revile her now as Dr. Dunlap had done.

But the older woman had become silent. She was standing with her ear to the wall and seemed to be intently listening to something. . . .

In another instant she sped to a shelf stacked with bars of soap and packages of detergent. Scurrying like a mother squirrel, she moved these objects aside, and presently uncovered a part of the wall where there was a small sliding panel. She cautioned Candy to silence, holding her finger to her lips, then slid the panel open and put her face to the aperture. After a few seconds she turned back toward Candy with a bemused smile on her face. "There he is!" she whispered ecstatically.

Candy stepped to the opening, which seemed to have been intended for a movie-projector window, and found herself gazing down into a good-sized amphitheater. The vast room was empty save for Dr. Dunlap, who was sitting under a strong light in the very center, and Krankeit himself, standing high in the uppermost tier of seats and barely discernible in the shadows.

Dr. Dunlap had a device of some sort clamped to his head: there were electrodes taped to his temples, and wires from them led to a screen coated with some fluorescent material, which stood a few feet before him. On the screen danced a jagged pattern of lines—wave lengths of the electrical impulses of his brain, apparently—and the distinguished-looking doctor, leaning forward slightly, stared wide-eyed at them as if hypnotized.

"Can you give me an 'all-clear?' " called Krankeit tersely, a small megaphone raised to his mouth.

"All clear!" replied Dunlap, tight-lipped.

"Ready for your little *standby?*" demanded Krankeit.

"Ready for little *standby!*" snapped Dunlap.

Krankeit leaned over into space, his keen eyes riveted to the patterned screen and the flashing instrument panel, as he lifted the miniature megaphone to his lips again.

"Ready for your little *countdown?*"

"Ready for little *countdown!*"

Krankeit regarded his wristwatch, stared at the sweeping second-hand.

"8... 7... stand by for standby... 6... ready for ready ... 5... 4... *stand by!* ... 3... 2... 1! Ready for your big *standby?*" He was practically shouting now, and both men had the intensity of children at a game of magic.

"Ready for big standby!"

"Ready for your big countdown?"

"Ready for big countdown!"

"Stand by!" shouted Krankeit, and, as he continued, his voice took on an odd metallic quality as though it were coming through a large public-address system: "100... 99... 98... 97... 96... 95... 94... 93... 92... 91... 90... 89... 88... 87... 86... 85... 84... 83... 82... 81... 80... 79... 78... 77... 76... 75... 74... 73... 72... 71... 70... 69... 68... 67... 66... 65... 64... 63... 62... 61... 60... 59... 58... 57... 56... 55... 54... 53... 52... 51... 50... 49... 48... 47... 46... 45... 44... 43... 42... 41... 40... 39... 38... 37... 36... 35... 34... 33... 32... 31... 30... 29... 28... 27... 26... 25... 24... 23... 22... 21... 20... 19... 18... 17... 16... 15... 14... 13... 12... 11... 10... 9... 8... 7... 6... 5!... 4!... 3!... 2!... 1. ...

JACK OFF!"

Stationed at her tiny window, Candy looked on incredulously at what took place when Krankeit's thunderous com-

mand had ceased echoing in the amphitheater. After a minute she turned weakly from the wall and said, "I think I'd
better leave now, if you don't mind. I'm afraid I'm getting
a bit of a headache."

"Don't forget what I told you," said Krankeit's mother,
eying her pugnaciously. "*Leave Irving alone!*"

She wandered again in the maze of white corridors, trying to find her way back to the sickroom. Walking slowly,
she considered the outlandish things that had been happening to her—the scene with Dr. Dunlap, the strange
meeting with Mrs. Semite, and now, this upsetting incident she'd witnessed in the amphitheater. She'd heard
about Krankeit's unprecedented theories from the nurse,
of course, but seeing them put to practice had been something of a shock. She was disturbed, bewildered, and, more
than anything else, she was terribly tired. She dabbed her
moist forehead with a hanky and wished she could sit
down. . . .

A few minutes later a burst of wild laughter, coming
from one of the rooms, told her where the others were.

She opened the door and was presented with the spectacle of Uncle Jack and Luther performing a primitive
dance together.

"Daddy" had gotten out of bed in his bathrobe and tur-
ban of bandages, and he and Luther were grunting and
shuffle-stamping about each other in American Indian
style. Luther was in his undershirt, and from time to
time, would lock his hands behind his neck and do an
obscene wiggle like a burlesque dancer. It was the sight of
this bald little roly-poly man doing bumps and grinds

in his undershirt that was provoking Livia's hilarious shrieking.

Obviously, they hadn't waited for Candy to return with the ice cubes to begin their merrymaking.

Seated in a corner, Aunt Ida—insanely calm—was reading a hospital-bound copy of *Popular Mechanics*.

When they saw Candy standing in the doorway, the men abruptly ceased their barbaric squirming and changed to a chaste and stately minuet. Uncle Jack bowing sedately and fat little Luther doing a charming curtsy.

"Too much! Too *much!*" Livia howled, falling on the bed helplessly.

Good Grief! Candy thought. They've gotten completely hysterical!

The two men soon tired of doing the minuet and reverted to their primitive technique—Luther scuffling around the room on his knees, Uncle Jack war-whooping and stamping his feet.

Just then the door opened and Krankeit entered.

To everyone's surprise, he didn't seem to be shocked by what was happening, and actually waved his hand to the dancers as if to tell them not to bother about him but to go on with their fun.

Perhaps it was for *her* sake, Candy thought with a catch in her throat, to save *her* from the painful embarrassment of a scene.

In gratitude for Krankeit's good sportsmanship, Uncle Jack and Luther linked arms like chorus girls and began kicking rhythmically to the tune "Give My Regards to Broadway."

The young doctor smiled good-naturedly, but refused

to go as far as taking part himself when Luther beckoned him to come and join the chorus line.

"I take it back!" Livia cried gaily to Krankeit from the bed. "I thought you were going to be one of those melancholy ones, but you're not a bad chap at all—God, if there's one thing depresses me it's to have some mopey Hebe around when people are trying to be cheerful, don't you agree?"

At this remark, a nervous tic appeared in Krankeit's cheek, but he soon mastered it and said to Uncle Jack, "Well, I'm glad to see you're up out of bed and getting the kinks out of your bones. Mustn't overdo it though. Mustn't take on too much the first day. . . . Careful your bandage doesn't come off. . . ."

Uncle Jack's dressing *had* come undone, and he was waving a loose yard of gauze, can-can style, in time to the step. Now, with amusing versatility, he changed again, metamorphosing into a gorilla—lumbering about, scratching himself under the arms, and pouting his lips disdainfully.

"Sid has become a real *scream* since he got that bang in the head," Livia commented.

The "ape" lurched to where Ida, deathly pale, was still reading *Popular Mechanics;* gripping her magazine tightly, she kept her eyes trained on the page and did not look up.

Uncle Jack made an insulting monkey-face in her direction, and turned to the wall. He seemed to be making some rapid adjustments in his costume. From time to time, he made a soft hooting sound in imitation of a chimpanzee. Then, finally ready, he turned to face the crowd

—he had undone his bathrobe, lifted his nightgown, and, with a fatuous leer, was exposing his member!

Good Lord! Candy thought in panic. *Not again!*

"You can't say he's not the life of the party," Livia quipped in high spirits.

Poor Luther, who had taken one brief look at what was happening, had buried his face in a chair, like an ostrich.

Uncle Jack stood not more than two feet from Ida and cynically waved his member at her. At last she looked up from her magazine. "Well—uh—well, perhaps something should be done," she suggested in a discreetly unruffled voice, catching Krankeit's eye.

"Oh my no!" Krankeit declared, with a scowl of professional concern.

"Well, after all—I mean don't you think—uh—" (The ape-man was *very* close to her. His gross organ virtually loomed in the corner of her sight.)

"Oh heavens no!" Krankeit assured her. "Perfectly okay. Best thing in the world for him."

"Dr. Krankeit feels that the way to clear up our mental problems is to . . . to *masturbate,* Aunt Ida," Candy explained.

Ida listened to this information calmly, but she had become rather green and was swallowing continuously.

"AH!"

Everyone turned and looked at Livia, who had suddenly staggered to her feet. She held her palm to her mouth as if to suppress a screech of fright, and, with the other hand, she pointed an accusing finger at Uncle Jack's member.

"*JACK!* . . . *AH!*" she gasped in certain recognition—and crumbled to the floor.

Uncle Jack and Luther set to work immediately to mimic her—falling and getting up in a series of imitations of people passing out from drink.

"Great Scott!" Krankeit exclaimed, looking at Livia lying motionless on the floor. "We'd better get her to the dispensary at once! I'm afraid she's had a bit *too much*," and, signifying to the others to continue with their fun, he lifted the unconscious young woman onto the wheeling-table and rolled her smoothly away.

Now that their audience was gone, and with Candy and Ida glaring at them, the two men finally stopped their cavorting and sat down exhausted on the bed.

"Whew!" panted Luther, trying to make it seem as if their insensate exhibition had been an innocent lark, "I don't know when I've had a workout like that in the last six years." He chuckled and glanced sheepishly at the women, who looked back at him in grim silence. "Well, Sidney," he said, getting up and retrieving his shirt from the floor, "this has been an awfully pleasant visit, and I hope—uh—I hope we've helped you get your mind off your troubles a bit—"

"Wait a minute!" Uncle Jack said excitedly, and sprang from the bed. "I just thought of one we forgot to do!" and he began to hum the familiar strains of the Parisian "Apache Dance," took several ominous strides, and froze ludicrously, having just knocked an imaginary Mademoiselle to the floor. "Right?" he said to Luther. "Come on!" he roared. "LET'S GO!" motioning for the chubby Luther to perform the painful role of the girl.

"Now Sidney, maybe we'd better not get started again," Luther observed apprehensively. "You know the doctor just told you to take it easy—"

"COME ON!" Uncle Jack bellowed, and whether he was furious at his partner's reluctance, or whether it was simply part of the dance, he stalked up to his brother-in-law and slapped him smartly in the face.

This was too much for Ida, who finally passed to the attack and began pushing Uncle Jack vigorously toward his bed.

"Hands off!" he shouted in astonished protest. "Hands off, you sow!"

I can't stand another minute of this, Candy thought. Good Grief! And she rushed blindly out of the room to find help.

She flew down the hall, and with a little sob of despair, flung open the first door she came to, but was startled to find herself again in the service room, full of mops and buckets, where she'd made the acquaintance of Irving Krankeit's mother.

It seemed impossible . . . she could have sworn that the tiny room was whole floors and corridors distant, tucked away in some obscure corner of the colossal building. Hadn't it taken her ten minutes to find her way back from it to Daddy's room?

She stepped to the shelf and moved aside some packages of detergent. . . . Yes, there was the little sliding panel!

It was still partially open, and as she looked she heard someone in the amphitheater say something that sounded like "Ping!" Candy had an almost physical premonition warning her not to look; but some still louder inner force fiercely compelled her to peer into the vastness below. . . .

"Chiang!"

Aunt Livia—naked, unconscious, attached by the wrists to the vertical operating table—looked like a handsome animal offered for sacrifice.

Seated immediately behind her was Krankeit. The young doctor sat silently as if meditating on the form before him, then he took something from a table at his side, leaned forward, and inserted it in Livia's girlish right buttock.

"Moo!" he said distinctly, settling back into his seat.

This was Krankeit's "ancient Chinese therapy," Candy thought, with a tinge of reverence. These were the Chinese pins with which he had treated *her*, the same silver pins. . . .

"Dung!"

. . . that he was now sticking in Livia.

Candy suddenly felt very tired; and beyond the fatigue was an aching uneasiness which wasn't due solely to her resentment at seeing Livia occupy *her* place on the tilting-table. . . . I feel as if something were coming to an end, she thought. My childhood perhaps. . . .

"Tch'ou!" Krankeit said, and sat back.

In a minute though, he was forward again with another pin. Back and forth he went, like someone giving artificial respiration very slowly; and the pins grew into clusters like two little bouquets, one on each of Livia's handsome tushy. . . .

"Moung!"

How defenseless Aunt Livia looked! . . . Strapped to the table, naked and unconscious . . . and a few hours ago it had been *her*. Of course Krankeit was a doctor, Candy reflected, but he was also a man! And Livia *was* beautiful. It seemed so unfair somehow, and Candy had a momentary impulse to take off her own things and rush into the amphitheater.

"Ping!"

Oh I just wish that it would stop happening! she thought, cross and weary. I just wish I were someplace else. . . .

"Meeow!" (There was a note of tense excitement in Krankeit's voice now which grew stronger with each pin.)

. . . someplace far from Racine. . . . I'm tired of that darn old college too.

"Fu!" Krankeit cried. "Feng! Jao!" (putting in three pins in quick succession).

"I don't *care*," Candy said to herself, "I don't want to see Aunt Livia anymore . . . or Dr. Krankeit either."

"Wowee!"

One of Krankeit's hands, Candy noticed, was briskly engaged in his lap. Why—why he's *abusing* himself, she thought, her eyebrows shooting up.

At that precise moment, she thought of New York City, and decided to go there . . .

"Wu Shih! Wu Shih!" Krankeit yelled.

. . . someplace where she knew no one, and where no one knew her . . .

"POW! FANG DANG POW!" Krankeit screamed triumphantly, dropping forward from his chair, to lie utterly spent, face down and apparently unconscious, on the floor of the great amphitheater.

. . . where she could lose the old Candy in the nameless city streets, she thought, where she could finally . . . be *herself*.

ten

10

There was only one tree on Grove Street. This was the sort of thing Candy was quick to notice, and to love. "Look," she would say softly, squeezing someone's hand. "Isn't it too *much!* I could just hug myself everytime I pass it!"

And that was where she met the hunchback.

It was late one airless summer day, when the sky over Greenwich Village was the color of lead. It had just begun to rain, and Candy was standing back in a shallow doorway, waiting for her bus. Dreamily humming a little Elizabethan tune, feeling fresh and quietly joyful in her new mandarin rain-cloak, hugging it to her—she saw him. He was out in the midst of the downpour, leaning against the tree, staring into the window display of the men's shop on the corner. He was standing very still, though from time to time there seemed to be a slight movement of his back, as if he might be consciously pressing his hump against the tree.

Candy's humming softened as she watched him, and her heart beat a little faster. *Oh, the fullness of it!* she thought, *the terrible, beautiful fullness of life!* And a great mass of feeling rose in her throat at the pity she felt for her father so shut away from it all, never to know life, never even to suspect what it was all about. She put her arms around her delightful body and hugged herself, so glad at being alive, really alive, and her eyes brimmed with shimmering gratitude.

Just then two boys passed the corner, dark coats turned up, heads half hidden out of the rain. One of them noticed the hunchback and gave a derisive snort:

"Wha'cha doin', Mac—gittin' yer nuts off?"

He kept nudging his companion, who wouldn't even bother to look.

"The guy's gittin' his *nuts* off fer chrissake!" he shouted again as they walked on.

The hunchback gazed after them oddly.

"Rubatubdub!" he said. "Rubadubtub!"

Candy hadn't heard either one of them distinctly, but there was no mistaking the tone of contempt, the obvious effort to hurt and humiliate. "The ignorant fools!" she said half aloud, and gave a little stamp of impatience. At that moment the bus rounded the corner beyond; she frowned as she watched it approach, but just before it reached her, she took a deep breath and walked away from the stop, then casually over to where the hunchback was standing.

"*Hi!*" she said, giving him a wonderfully warm smile and tossing back the hood of her cloak to feel the fresh rain on her face. . . . Wasn't it just too much, she thought joyfully, standing here in the rain, in Greenwich Village, talking to a hunchback—when she *should* have been at her job ten minutes ago! . . . She considered the explanation she would have to give, the attempt to make them understand, and she was so happy and proud of herself she could have wept.

"That's *my* tree, you know," she said instead, smiling like a mischievous child, then laughing gaily at her own foolishness. "I pretend that it is," she admitted, almost shyly. "The *only* tree on Grove Street! Oh, I do love it so!" She leaned forward and touched it gently, half closing her eyes, and then she gave the hunchback another tender smile.

The shop on this corner of Grove was a man's underwear shop, and the hunchback's eyes devoured another crotch or two before he looked up. He was also smiling. He supposed she was a policewoman. *"Rubatubdub!"* he said, agitating his hump vigorously against the tree. Getting run in was part of his kick.

"Three men in a tub!" cried Candy, laughing in marvel at their immediate rapport. How simple! she thought. How wonderfully, beautifully simple the important things are! And how it had so completely escaped her father! She would have given twenty years of her life to have shared the richness of this moment with her father—he who had said that poems were "impractical"! The poor darling dummy! Why *only* a poem could capture it! Only a poem could trap the elusiveness, the light-like subtlety, the vapor-edge of a really big thing, and lead it, coax it past . . . a poem, or music perhaps . . . yes, of course, music. And she began to hum softly, swaying her body a little, her fingers distractedly caressing the tree. She felt very relaxed with the hunchback.

And he was still smiling too—but that first gray glimmer of hope had died from his eyes, and they narrowed a bit now as he decided, quite simply, that she was a nut.

"Hungry," he said, pointing to his mouth, *"hungry."*

"Oh!" cried Candy, suddenly remembering, and she reached into the pocket of her cloak and took out a small paper bag. It was a bag of bread crumbs; she carried it often for pigeons in Washington Square. "I have this," she said, her wide eyes beautifully blue and ingenuous. She helped herself first, to show that it wasn't mere charity, but rather a human experience, simple, warm, and shared.

There was something disconcerting though in the way this hunchback sniggered, rolling his eyes, and squirmed against the tree, wiping his mouth with the back of his hand; but, after a moment, he took some of the crumbs too.

"Rubatubdub!" he said.

Candy laughed. She heard a wisdom and complex symbology in the hunchback's simple phrases. It was as though she were behind the scenes of something like the Dadaist movement, even creatively a part of it. This was the way things happened, she thought, the really big things, things that ten years later change the course of history, just this way, on the street corners of the Village; and here she was, a part of it. How incredibly ironic that her father would have thought she was "wasting her time"! The notion made her throat tighten and her heart rise up in sorrow for him.

"You got quarter, lady?" asked the hunchback then, nodding his head in anticipation. He held out his hand, but Candy was already shaking her curls defensively and fumbling in her purse.

"No, I don't think I have a *cent*, darn it! Here's an Athenean florin," she said, holding up a lump of silver, then dropping it back into the purse, "550 B.C. . . . *that* won't do us any good, will it? Not unless we're Sappho and Pythagoras and don't know it!" And she looked up, closing her purse and shaking her head, happily, as though not having any money herself would actually make them closer.

"*Are* you Pythagoras?" she asked gaily.

"You get your rubadub, don't you lady?" muttered the hunchback as he started shuffling away. *"Fuckashitpiss! Fuckashitpiss! Rubadub, rubadub!"*

This struck Candy with such anxiety that for a moment she was speechless. She could not bear the idea of his going away angry, and also in the back of her mind was the pride she would feel if, in a few days, she could be walking down the street with Ted and Harold, or with one of the people from International House, and the hunchback would speak to her by name; they might even stop and chat a bit, and she would introduce him:

"Ted, this is my friend Derek," or whatever; it could certainly be as important as Blind Battersea, the sightless beggar in Washington Park, being able to recognize Ted's voice.

"Listen," she cried, hurrying after him, "if you don't mind potluck, we could have something at my place—it's just past the corner here—I know there are some eggs. . . ."

When Candy had slipped out of her cloak and kicked off her shoes, she went into the bathroom. "Won't be a min-

ute," she said, and very soon she reappeared, rubbing her
hair with a towel, fluffing it out, her head back, eyes half
closed for the moment as she stood there in the middle of
the room.

"I don't know which is best," she said with a luxurious
sigh, "the freshness of rain . . . or the warmth of fire."

She had changed into a loose flannel shirt and a pair of
tight-fitting faded bluejeans which were rolled up almost
to the knee. She had another towel draped across her
shoulder, and she laid this on the arm of the hunchback's
chair as she crossed the room.

"Take off some of your things if you want," she said
airily, "let them dry by the radiator," and she sat down
on the edge of the couch opposite him and rubbed her
feet with the towel, doing this carefully and impersonally,
as though they were pieces of priceless china which belonged to someone else, yet silhouetting the white curve
of her bare legs against the black corduroy couch-cover,
and exclaiming genially: "My feet are soaked! Aren't
yours?" She didn't wait for an answer, nor seemed to expect one, only wanting to maintain a casual chatter to put
the hunchback at ease; she took care not to look at him
directly, as she stood up and crossed the room again, indicating with a gesture the magazine stand near his chair:
"There's a *PR* and *Furioso* there—if you feel like light
reading. I'm afraid there's not much else at the moment—
I'll just get us a drink." And she disappeared then into the
tiny kitchen.

The hunchback had been sniggering and squirming
about in the chair, and now finally he picked up the towel

and wiped his face, then blew his nose into it and spat several times.

"Rubatubtub!" he muttered.

Candy's gay laugh rang from the kitchen.

"Wish we had something stronger," she called out, "we could use it after that rain." Then she came in with a large bottle of Chianti and two glasses already filled, and set these on the table. "Help yourself to more," she said, taking a sip of hers. "Umm, good," she said, and went back into the kitchen, "won't be a minute . . . well, not more than *five*, anyway." She had turned on the phono—some Gregorian chants—and hummed along with the music now as she busied herself, coming in and out, setting the table, and keeping up a spritely monologue the while.

The hunchback had a sip of the wine and spat it in the towel.

Through the open door of the kitchen, Candy could be seen moving about, and now she was bending over to put something into the oven. In the tight jeans, her round little buttocks looked so firm and ripe that any straight-thinking man would have rushed in at once to squeeze and bite them; but the hunchback's mind was filled with freakish thoughts. From an emotional stand-point, he would rather have been in the men's room down at Jack's Bar on the Bowery, eating a piece of urine-soaked bread while thrusting his hump against someone from the Vice Squad. And yet, though he had decided that she was nutty (and because of this she was of no use to his ego), he was also vaguely aware that she was a mark; and, in an obscure, obstacle-strewn way, he was trying to think about this now: *how to get the money*. He wasn't too good at it, however, for his sincerity of thought was not direct enough: he didn't really feel he *needed* money, but rather that he *should* feel he needed it. It was perhaps the last vestige of normalcy in the hunchback's values; it only cropped up now and then.

"Onion omelet," Candy announced with a flourish as she entered, "hope you like tarragon and lots of garlic," and she put it on the table. "Looks good, doesn't it?" She felt she could say this last with a certain innocent candor, because her friends assured her she was a very good cook.

Aside from an occasional grunt and snort, the hunchback kept silent throughout the meal and during Candy's lively commentary, while into his image-laden brain now and then shot the primal questions: *"Where? No kill! How? Without kill! Where?"*

This silence of his impressed Candy all the more, making her doubly anxious to win his approval. "Oh, but here I'm talking away a mile, and you can't get in a single word!" She beamed, and nodded with a show of wisdom, "Or isn't it really that there's nothing to say—'would it have been worth while *after all,* et cetera, et cetera.' Yes, *I* know . . . oh, there's the tea now. *Tea!* Good night, *I'm* still on Eliot—the darling old fuddy, don't you *love* him? It's coffee, of course. Espresso. I won't be a minute. . . . Have some of the Camembert, not too *bien fait,* I'm afraid, but . . ." She rushed out to the kitchen, still holding her napkin, while the hunchback sat quietly, munching his bread. It was hardly the first time he had been involved in affairs of this sort.

When the darling girl returned, she suggested they move over to the couch to have their coffee. There she sat close beside him and leafed through a book of Blake's reproductions.

"Aren't they a *groove*," she was saying, "they're *so* funny! Most people don't get it at all!" She looked up at the wall opposite, where another print was hanging, and said gleefully: "And don't you just love *that* one? The details, I mean, did you ever look at it closely? Let me get it."

The print was hanging by a wire placed high, and Candy had to reach. She couldn't quite get it at first, and for a long moment she was standing there, lithe and lovely, stretching upward, standing on the tiptoes of one foot, the other out like a ballet-dancer's. As she strained higher, she felt the sinews of her calf rounding firmly and the edge of her flannel shirt lifting gently above her waist and upward across her bare back, while the muscles of her darling little buttocks tightened and thrust out taut beneath the jeans. Oh, I *shouldn't!* she thought, making another last effort to reach the print. What if he thinks I'm . . . well, it's *my* fault, darn it!

As it happened, the hunchback *was* watching her and, with the glimpse of her bare waist, it occurred to him suddenly, as though the gray sky itself had fallen, that, as for the other girls who had trafficked with him, what they had wanted was to be ravenously desired—to be so overwhelmingly physically needed that, despite their every effort to the contrary for a real and spiritual rapport, their beauty so powerfully, undeniably asserted itself as to reduce the complex man to simple beast . . . who must be fed.

By the time Candy had the print down and had reached

the couch with it, the eyes of the hunchback were quite changed; they seemed to be streaked with red now, and they were very bright. The precious girl noticed it at once, and she was a little flustered as she sat down, speaking rapidly, pointing to the print: "Isn't this too *much?* Look at this figure, here in the corner, most people don't even . . ." She broke off for a moment to cough and blush terribly as the hunchback's eyes devoured her, glistening. In an effort to regain composure, she touched her lovely curls and gave a little toss of her head. 'What *can* he be thinking?' she asked herself. 'Well, it's my own fault, darn it!' The small eyes of the hunchback blazed; he was thinking of *money.* "I love you!" he said then quickly, the phrase sounding odd indeed.

"Oh, darling, *don't* say that!" said Candy, imploring, as though she had been quite prepared, yet keeping her eyes down on the book.

"I want very much!" he said, touching her arm at the elbow.

She shivered just imperceptibly and covered his hand with her own. "You mustn't say that," she said with softness and dignity.

"*I want fuck you!*" he said, putting his other hand on her pert left breast.

She clasped his hand, holding it firmly, as she turned to him, her eyes closed, a look of suffering on her face. "No, darling, please" she murmured and she was quite firm.

"I want fuck——suck you!" he said, squeezing the breast while she felt the sweet little nipple reaching out like a tiny mushroom.

She stood up abruptly, putting her hands to her face.

"Don't. Please don't," she said. She stood there a moment, then walked to the window. "Oh why must it be like this?" she beseeched the dark sky of the failing day. "Why? Why?" She turned and was about to repeat it, but the voice of the hunchback came first.

"Is because of *this?*" he demanded. "Because of *this?*" He was sitting there with a wretched expression on his face, and one arm raised and curled behind his head, pointing at his hump.

Candy came forward quickly, like a nurse in emergency. "*No,* you poor darling, of course it isn't! *No, no,*" and the impetus of her flight carried her down beside him again and put him in her arms. "You silly darling!" She closed her eyes, leaning her face against his as she stroked his head. "I hadn't even noticed," she said.

"Why, then?" he wanted to know. "*Why?*"

Now that she had actually touched him, she seemed more at ease. "*Why?*" she sighed. "Oh, I don't know. Girls are like that, never quite knowing what they want—or need. Oh, I don't know, I want it to be *perfect,* I guess."

"Because of *this,*" repeated the hunchback, shrugging heavily.

"No, you darling," she cooed, insisting, closed-eyed again, nudging his cheek with her nose, "no, no, no. What earthly *difference* does it make! I have blue eyes—you have that. What possible earthly difference does it make?"

"*Why?*" he demanded, reaching up under her shirt to grasp one of her breasts, then suddenly pulling her brassiere up and her shoulder back, and thrusting forward to cover the breast with his mouth. Candy sobbed, "*Oh darling, no,*" but allowed her head to recline gently against the couch. "Why does it have to be like this?" she pleaded. "Why? Oh, I know it's my own fault, darn it." And she let him kiss and suck her breast, until the nipple became terribly taut and she began to tingle all down through her precious tummy, then she pulled his head away, cradling it in her arms, her own eyes shimmering with tears behind a brave smile. "No, darling," she implored, *"please . . .* not now."

"Because of *this,*" said the hunchback bitterly.

"No, no, no," she cried, closing her eyes and hugging the head to her breast, holding his cheek against it, but trying to keep his mouth from the proud little nipple, "no, no, *not* because of that!"

"I want!" said the hunchback, with one hand on her hip now undoing the side buttons of her jeans; then he swiftly forced the hand across the panty sheen of her rounded tummy and down into the sweet damp.

"Oh, darling, no!" cried the girl, but it was too late, without making a scene, for anything to be done; his stubby fingers were rolling the little clitoris like a marble in oil. Candy leaned back in resignation, her heart too big to deprive him of this if it meant so much. With her head closed-eyed, resting again on the couch, she would endure it as long as she could. But, before she reached the saturation point, he had nuzzled his face down from her breast across her bare stomach and into her lap, bending his arm forward to force down her jeans and panties as he did, pulling at them on the side with his other hand.

"No, no, darling!" she sighed, but he soon had them down below her knees, at least enough so to replace his fingers with his tongue.

It means so much to him, Candy kept thinking, *so much*, as he meanwhile got her jeans and panties down completely so that they dangled now from one slender ankle as he adjusted her legs and was at last on the floor himself in front of her, with her legs around his neck, and his mouth very deep inside the fabulous honeypot.

"If it means so much," Candy kept repeating to herself, until she didn't think she could bear it another second, and she wrenched herself free, saying *"Darling, oh darling,"* and seized his head in her hands with a great show of passion.

"Oh, why?" she begged, holding his face in her hands, looking at him mournfully. "Why?"

"I need fuck you!" said the hunchback huskily. He put his face against the upper softness of her marvelous bare leg. Small, strange sounds came from his throat.

"Oh, darling, darling," the girl keened pitifully, "I can't bear your crying." She sighed, and smiled tenderly, stroking his head.

"I *think* we'd better go into the bedroom," she said then, her manner suddenly prim and efficient.

In the bathroom, standing before the glass, Candy finished undressing—unbuttoning her shirt, slowly, carefully, a lamb resigned to the slaughter, dropping the shirt to the floor, and taking off her brassiere, gradually revealing her nakedness to herself, with a little sigh, almost of wistful regret, at how *very* lovely she was, and at how her nipples grew and stood out like cherrystones, as they always did when she watched herself undress. How he *wants* me! she thought. Well, it's my own fault, darn it! And she tried to imagine the raging lust that the hunchback felt for her as she touched her curls lightly. Then she cast a last glimpse at herself in the glass, blushing at her own loveliness, and trembling slightly at the very secret notion of this beauty-and-beast sacrifice, she went back into the bedroom.

The hunchback was lying naked, curled on his side like a big foetus, when Candy appeared before him, standing for a moment in full lush radiance, a naked angel bearing the supreme gift. Then, she got into bed quickly, under the sheet, almost soundlessly, saying, *"Darling, darling,"* and cuddling him to her at once, while he, his head filled with the most freakish thoughts imaginable—all about tubs of living and broken toys, every manner of excrement, scorpions, steelwool, pig-masks, odd metal harness, etc.—tried desperately to pry into the images a single reminder: *the money!*

"Do you want to kiss me some more, darling?" asked the girl with deadly soft seriousness, her eyes wide, searching his own as one would a child's. Then she sighed and lay back, slowly taking the sheet from her, again to make him the gift of all her wet, throbbing treasures, as he, glazed-eyed and grunting, slithered down beside her.

"Don't hurt me, darling," she murmured, as in a dream, while he parted the exquisitely warm round thighs with his great head, his mouth opening the slick lips all sugar and glue, and his quick tongue finding her pink candy clit at once.

"Oh, darling, darling," she said, stroking his head gently, watching him, a tender courageous smile on her face.

The hunchback put his hands under her, gripping the foam-rubber balls of her buttocks, and sucked and nibbled

her tiny clit with increasing vigor. Candy closed her eyes
and gradually raised her legs, straining gently upward now,
dropping her arms back by her head, one to each side, pretending they were pinioned there, writhing slowly, sobbing
—until she felt she was no longer giving, but was on the
verge of taking, and, as with an effort, she broke her hands
from above her and grasped the hunchback's head and
lifted it to her mouth, coming forward to meet him, kissing
him deeply. "Come inside me, darling," she whispered urgently, "I want you *inside* me!"

The hunchback, his brain seething with pure strange-
ness, hardly heard her. He had forgotten about the money,
but did know that *something* was at stake, and his head was
about to burst in trying to recall what it was. Inside his
mind was like a gigantic landslide of black eels, billions of
them, surging past, one of which held the answer. His job:
catch it! Catch it, and chew off the top of its head; and
there, in the gurgling cup, would be . . . the *message:*
"You have forgotten about. . . ?"

But which eel was it? While his eyes grew wilder and
rolled back until only the whites showed, Candy, thinking
that he was beside himself with desire for her, covered his
face with sweet wet kisses, until he suddenly went stiff in
her arms as his racing look stopped abruptly on the floor
near the bed: it was a coat hanger, an ordinary wire coat
hanger, which had fallen from the closet, and the hunchback flung himself out of the bed and onto the floor, clutching the hanger to him feverishly. Then, as in a fit of bitter
triumph, he twisted it savagely into a single length of
coiled black wire, and gripping it so tightly that his entire

body shook for a moment, he lunged forward, one end of it locked between his teeth. *He thought it was the eel.*

Candy had started up, half sitting now, one hand instinctively to her pert, pulsating breast.

"Darling, what is it?" she cried. "Darling, you *aren't* going to . . ."

The hunchback slowly rose, as one recovered from a seizure of apoplexy, seeming to take account of his surroundings anew, and, just as he had learned from the eel's head that the forgotten issue was money, so too he believed now that the girl wanted to be beaten.

"*Why,* darling?" pleaded Candy, curling her lovely legs as the hunchback slowly raised the black wire snake above his head. "*Why? Why?*" she cried.

And as he began to strike her across the back of her legs, she sobbed, "Oh, why, darling, why?" her long round limbs twisting, as she turned and writhed, her arms back beside her head as before, moving too except at the wrist where they were as stiff as though clamped there with steel, and she was saying: "Yes! *Hurt* me! Yes, yes! Hurt me as *they* have hurt you!" and now her ankles as well seemed secured, shackled to the spot, as she lay, spread-eagled, sobbing piteously, straining against her invisible bonds, her lithe round body arching upward, hips circling slowly, mouth wet, nipples taut, her teeny piping clitoris distended and throbbing, and her eyes glistening like fire, as she devoured all the penitence for each injustice ever done to hunchbacks of the world; and as it continued she slowly opened her eyes, that all the world might see the tears there—but instead she herself saw, through the rise and fall of the wire lash—the hunchback's white gleaming hump! The *hump,* the white, unsunned forever, radish-root white of hump, and it struck her, more sharply than the wire whip, as something she had seen before—the naked, jutting buttocks, upraised in a sexual thrust, not a thrust of taking, but of *giving,* for it had been an image in a hospital room mirror, of her own precious buttocks, naked and upraised, gleaming white, and thrusting downwards, as she had been made to do in giving herself to her Uncle Jack!

With a wild impulsive cry, she shrieked: *"Give me your hump!"*

The hunchback was startled for a moment, not comprehending.

"Your *hump,* your *hump!*" cried the girl, "GIVE ME YOUR HUMP!"

The hunchback hesitated, and then lunged headlong toward her, burying his hump between Candy's legs as she hunched wildly, pulling open her little labias in an absurd effort to get it in her.

"Your hump! Your hump!" she kept crying, scratching and clawing at it now.

"Fuck! Shit! Piss!" she screamed. "Cunt! Cock! Crap! Prick! Kike! Nigger! Wop! *Hump!* HUMP!" and she teetered on the blazing peak of pure madness for an instant . . . and then dropped down, slowly, through gray and grayer clouds into a deep, soft, black, night.

When Candy awoke she was alone. She lay back, thinking over the events of the afternoon. Well, it's my own fault, darn it, she sighed, then smiled a little smile of forgiveness at herself—but this suddenly changed to a small frown, and she sat up in bed, cross as a pickle. *"Darn it!"* she said aloud, and with real feeling, for she had forgotten to have them exchange names.

eleven

//

After freshening up a bit, Candy left the apartment and started walking down West 4th Street. The rain had stopped, and a cool gentle breeze was blowing; apparently it was going to be a lovely evening indeed.

It was too late now of course to think about the job; in fact, it was almost dark when she reached the corner of Sixth Avenue, and she decided, quite on impulse, to stop in at the Riviera and have a Pernod.

Jack Katt and Tom Smart were there, at a front table, lushing it up and keen for puss. These were two fellows whom Candy vaguely knew and generally avoided. They were extraordinarily handsome and clever chaps, and Candy alone seemed immune to their undeniable charm; this was a constant source of annoyance to them. Now, when she entered, they graciously invited her to join them, but she refused. She wanted to sit quietly alone and cherish the memory of the past few hours with . . . but she *didn't* have the name to conjure with! And that was the blight on the experience, for she kept thinking of him now simply as "the hunchback," and every time the word formed in her mind she was cross enough with herself to bite. She didn't like thinking of him that way. What earthly difference could it make! she kept demanding, pouting her pretty mouth and clenching her small fist on the bar. Then she recalled the name she had given him, "Derek," and was happy with that for the moment, smiling again and sipping her drink.

"What the deuce is wrong with you?" asked the bartender suddenly, he who had been staring at the girl and had seen the gamut of emotions flit across her face.

"Nothing that *you* would understand," replied Candy imperiously; she didn't like the looks of this fellow, *nor* his forward manner. She lowered her eyes to the glass in her hand and quite ignored him; but he walked around the bar and looked frowningly down at the stool she was sitting on.

"Anything wrong?" Candy asked, and with an icy hauteur she knew would send a shiver up his spine.

"Apparently not," he replied easily, though without relaxing his consideration altogether. "Somehow, from the gamut of emotions which crossed your face, I had the idea the *stool* had slipped up into your *damp*."

"I beg your pardon?" said Candy, not comprehending, but even so not too keen on the fellow's tone.

"*You* know," insisted the bartender, going back behind the bar again, "your puss, your jelly-box . . . I thought the stool had somehow slipped up into your jelly-box. It happened the other night, a hefty babe was sitting here at the

bar . . . not on the stool you're on, but the next one, and
I was watching her. Well, she seemed to gradually *sink
down* toward the floor, you know, as though the stool itself
were going right through the floor, and . . . well, as I say,
I was watching her, and, by God, a veritable gamut of emotions was crossing her face while this was happening . . .
and what *had* happened was that somehow the stool had
slipped or pushed up into her jelly-box, right up inside it,
taking all the clothes with it, skirt, slip, panties and all,
right up into her *thing* . . . the whole seat of the stool and
about a foot of the legs. Christ, I never saw anything like it
before! Of course, she was a good deal heavier than *you,* in
fact, a lot heavier. She was a hefty babe, and . . ."

Candy didn't like this gabby intrusion into her thoughts
about Derek and the afternoon behind them, and she was
quick to let her expression reflect the annoyance she felt;
but she allowed him to ramble on, not following the words
at all, because she didn't care for this chap's tone. She supposed that he needed her in a way, but she wouldn't think
about that now, she was too full at the moment, too full
and warm from . . . she recalled Professor Mephesto's
words, "from this wonderful business of *living.*" She
thought of herself for the moment as a lovely, contented
cat . . . snuggled warm before the fire in her furabout,
purring happily; she could have hugged herself. Yet on another level she did feel that the general ambience of the
bar was somehow degrading to the experience of the afternoon, the experience she wanted so much to keep pure and
whole, to nurture and fondle, privately, as one might a
newborn babe of one's own. She knew that she should be
in a more *refined* place than this Riviera bar, and she

decided she would see if any good foreign films were playing at the local art movie-houses.

She went over to the table where Jack Katt and Tom
Smart were sitting and inquired. Of course they had no
notion of what was playing at the art cinemas, or anywhere
else for that matter, being out only for cheap strong lush
and slick tight puss. But they pretended they knew all
about the various programs and insisted that Candy sit
down while they discussed it. Then the suave Tom Smart
leaned forward and spoke confidingly to the girl: "I'd sure
like to dip my jumbo into that hot little honeypot of yours
tonight!"

"No, no," said Jack Katt, his dark fire-glint eyes flashing
with an impatience which would have made most girls
tingle and cream, "let me handle this!" And he tried to
pull the handsome Tom Smart away and at the same time
actually attempted to thrust his hand into Candy's sweet
little blouse.

"You silly boys!" she said crossly. She knew that this was
simply their way of expressing a need for her, but she
didn't care for this sort of talk at any time, and especially
not now when all her thoughts were with Derek.

"Good Christ Almighty," exclaimed Tom Smart, turning to his companion, *"will* you let me handle this! Now
you've offended her! Christ!"

"You!" shouted Jack Katt. "You and your damned
oblique approach! *I want puss!"*

And so they fell to arguing and discussing the tactic,
though to Candy it was a respite and she pursued her re-
flections on the hours past.

She hardly noticed when they were joined at the table a

few minutes later by another person, Dr. Howard Johns, a pleasant, middle-aged chap, certainly not the looker that Tom and Jack were, but perhaps more stable, and no doubt more comfortable for a young girl to be with. Nor did Candy catch his name at first, if in fact these two even troubled to introduce him, so informal were they in such matters.

"Listen, do you know what he is?" asked Tom Smart, after a minute, speaking to Candy. "A gynecologist! Ha-ha-ha!"

"Good Grief," said Candy.

"Sure," said Tom Smart, and turning to the doctor, went on in his winningly irrepressible way, "how would you like to look up *that* snatch, Doc? Boy, it's honey and cream!"

"It's a living snake!" said Jack Katt.

This seemed to embarrass the doctor somewhat and he shifted uneasily in his chair.

"Well," said Candy, "I've never met a . . . a gynecologist *socially*. How do you do?"

"Are *you* kidding?" shouted Tom Smart. "How does he *do?* He gets *more pussy* in three hours than most chaps do in a week! Right, Doc?"

"Now, really, Tom, Jack," said Dr. Johns, "I mean, fun is fun, but . . ." He was clearly upset about the turn the conversation had taken.

"I think you boys are terrible," said Candy indignantly, and she got up and went to another table.

"Good God!" cried Jack Katt. "Now you've lost that hot puss for us! Christ! Christ!"

"What! What!" said Tom Smart. "*I* lost it? Great Scott man, don't you realize that if . . ."

And so they would discuss it for hours on end.

Meanwhile, Dr. Johns got up and joined Candy at the other table.

"Well," he said, "they are certainly . . . certainly *outgoing* chaps, I must say. I'm terribly sorry about that. Really . . . I hardly . . ."

"Oh they're just silly boys," said Candy, "it's just their way of trying to . . . trying to *express* themselves . . . aesthetically, I suppose."

"Hmm," said Dr. Johns, glancing at them again. They were scuffling about the floor now, wallowing in the pools of beer and sawdust, shouting remarks about "tight quim," "hot puss," etc., etc.

Both Candy and the doctor looked away.

"Do you happen to know what's playing at the 5th Avenue Cinema?" she asked.

"No, I'm afraid I don't," said Dr. Johns. "Sorry."

"I'd like so much to see a good film tonight," said the girl.

"I don't go to the films much myself," he said. "Enjoy them, do you?"

"Well, of course, I only go to the art films," said Candy.

"I see," said Dr. Johns.

"Films like *The Quiet One,* and *The Cabinet of Dr. Caligari.*"

"Well," said Dr. Johns, "would you like me to go and get a paper for you? It would probably be listed there."

"Oh no," said Candy, "that's all right, thanks very much." She was pleased by his consideration.

"Are you sure?" he asked.

"Oh yes, thanks. I'm sure someone will come in who

knows what's playing there tonight. I know almost everyone who comes in here."

"I'm afraid I don't," said the doctor.

"Oh, you'll get to know them," said Candy, "they're all
swell kids."

"Yes, I'd like to," he said, rather dubiously. "Who is
your doctor . . . perhaps I know him."

"Well, I haven't been to a doctor since I've been in New
York . . . not to a gynecologist anyway. I'm not married,
of course, and . . . well, I suppose a single girl doesn't
need to go to a gynecologist very often, does she?" In spite
of her smile, the perfect girl was blushing.

Dr. Johns frowned.

"Well, of course, you really should have a periodic check-
up," he said. "I mean certainly you should have that.
When was the last time you did?"

"Oh gracious," said Candy, trying to recall, "it must
have been a year ago at least."

"Far too long, far too long," said the doctor seriously.

"Gosh, guess *I'd* better make an appointment," said
Candy.

"Hmm. The difficulty is, you see, I'm off on two months'
holiday starting tomorrow," said Dr. Johns. He looked
around the bar. "I'll tell you what," he said, getting up
from the table, "I won't be a moment," and he went out
the door.

Candy was humming the theme music of *Alexander
Nevsky,* one of her favorite movies, when Dr. Johns came
back in the bar, carrying a little black bag. He stopped at
the table and smiled at her. "We can give you an examination," he said, "just over there." And he assisted her up.

Candy was amazed. "Here? In the *Riviera?* Good Grief, I don't . . ."

"Oh yes," said Dr. Johns. "Just here . . . this will do nicely." He had led the girl to the door of the men's toilet, and quickly inside. It was extremely small, a simple cabinet with a stool, nothing more. He locked the door.

"Good Grief," said Candy, "I really don't think . . ."

"Oh yes," Dr. Johns assured her, "perfectly all right." He put his little bag down and started taking off her skirt. "Now we'll just slip out of these things," he said.

"Well, are you sure that . . ." Candy was quite confused.

"Now, the little panties," he said, pulling them down. "Lovely things you wear," he added and lifted her up onto the stool.

"Now you just stand with one foot on each side of the stool, limbs spread, that's right and . . . oh yes, you can brace yourself with your hands against the walls . . . yes, just so. . . . Fine!"

He bent quickly to his kit and took out a small clamp and inserted it between the girl's darling little labias, so that they were held apart.

"*Good!*" he said. "Now I just want to test these clitorial reflexes—often enough, that's where trouble strikes first." And he began to gently massage her sweet pink clit. "Can you feel that?"

"Good Grief yes!" said Candy, squirming about, "are you sure that this . . ."

"Hmm," said Dr. Johns. "Normal response there all right. Now I just want to test these clitorial reflexes to tactile surfaces." And he began sucking it wildly, clutching the precious girl to him with such sudden force and abandon that her feet slipped off the stool and into the well of it. During the tumult the flushing mechanism was set in motion and water now surged out over the two of them, flooding the tiny cabinet and sweeping out of it and into the bar.

There was a violent pounding at the door.

"What in God's name is going on in there?" demanded the manager, who had just arrived. He and the bartender were throwing their weight against the door of the cabinet which by now was two feet deep in water as the doctor and Candy thrashed about inside.

"Good Grief!" she kept saying. They had both fallen to the floor. The doctor was snorting and spouting water, trying desperately to keep sucking and yet not to drown.

Finally with a great lunge the two men outside broke open the door. They were appalled by the scene.

"Good God! Good God!" they shouted. "What in the name of God is going on here!"

A police officer arrived at that moment and was beside himself with rage at the spectacle.

The doctor had lost consciousness by the time he was pulled to his feet. Both he and Candy were sopping wet and completely disheveled. She was naked from the waist down.

"He's a doctor!" she cried to the policeman, who was dragging him about like a sack and pulling her by the arm.

"Uh-huh," said the cynical cop, "Dr. Caligari, I suppose."

Candy didn't like this kind of flippant reference to an

art film. "This *happens* to be an examination," she said with marked disdain.

"You can say *that* again, sister," said the officer, taking a good look himself.

"Good Grief!" said Candy, snatching the clamp out from between her labes.

The manager and the bartender were speechless with fury.

"*You . . . you . . .*" stammered the manager, shaking his finger at Candy.

"This so *happens* to be a private examination by my doctor!" said Candy with great haughtiness.

"*You are barred from the Riviera!*" he shouted with the finality of doom itself.

The doctor had regained consciousness now, but was still lost in his insane desire for the girl and flung himself against her in such ardor that they tumbled back into the cabinet with a splash, Candy shrieking, "Good Heavens!"

The policeman snatched them out again and drove them ahead of him with his club through the bar.

Near the door, still writhing about on the floor, were the two good-looking madcaps, Katt and Smart.

"*Augh,*" said the policeman in an expression of sheer disgust. And he struck a few blows at them with his stick as he might have at a reptile; but then he had to hurry on to see to his two prisoners.

"What the devil is he doing with that *stick?*" Jack Katt wanted to know, staring after them from where he lay in a great pool of stale beer.

"You poor sap," said Tom Smart, "he's going to put that stick in her honeypot, don't you know that?"

"Goddam it," shouted Jack Katt, "why didn't *we* bring such a stick as that! It's your fault, you swine!"

And so they fell to grappling about again in the mire of wet sawdust under their table.

On the street, Candy and the doctor were hustled into a patrol car, which departed with a roar.

twelve

12

In the police car, the two officers were wide-eyed at Candy's half-nakedness, as she still carried her skirt and pants in a dripping ball.

"Okay sister, cover it up!" said one of them brusquely.

"Good Night!" said Candy, "my things are soaking wet! How can I put *these on?*"

Dr. Johns, who had been securely pinioned in the corner of the back seat, suddenly lunged forward.

"Perfect!" he cried. "Perfect! Her tubes are *perfect!*"

"You've got a screw loose, buddy!" said one of the cops, giving the doctor a terrific blow on the head with his night-stick.

The car was plummeting down MacDougal Street, sirens wailing, so that Candy had to shout to make herself heard.

"Stop that! You can't hit him like that. Let me see your credentials. . . . I don't believe you're even police officers!"

"Here's a credential for you, momma!" said the officer in the back seat with her, and he tore open his fly and forced her hand inside. Candy flailed at him wildly with her free hand, half rising and falling against the driver in her desperation to escape the obscenity.

"Look out!" yelled the driver, for the girl had half obscured his view and interfered with his control of the machine—but it was too late, for at that moment a truck pulled out of a side street directly into their path.

"Christ! Christ!" shouted the driver, swerving the patrol car sharply, and with an agonizing scream of brakes the car careened hopelessly sideways past the truck, righted itself momentarily and then crashed headlong into the San Remo bar.

There were two hundred and seventy-five homosexuals in the bar at that particular moment, and they thought it was a raid. About half of them rushed insanely about trying to get out the doors, and the other half began beating in capering senseless frenzy on the car and the policemen.

"They're preverts!" shouted one policeman. "We'll have to blast our way out!"

In the confusion that followed, Candy found herself being pulled away from the scene by an unknown man.

"Quickly, quickly," he kept saying in an urgent whisper, and it was apparent he was helping her escape from the authorities. They were soon to Third Street, rushing down it toward Sixth Avenue.

"Oh, it's simply a nightmare!" Candy was saying as she ran along beside him, modestly trying to conceal her sweet nakedness. Then they were at the avenue and the strange man assisted her into a cab.

"The Cracker Foundation," he said to the driver, "and hurry!"

"Right!" said the driver, craning forward over the back seat for a moment, trying to see through the half-light of the cab into Candy's little honeypot.

"I'm putting on my things," exclaimed the girl, "wet or not! Good Grief!" And she began to get into them, the man beside her helping with the pants.

"Thanks," said Candy, feeling a good deal more secure once she had them on again, *"and* thanks for the rescue! Good Gosh, *I* thought we were going to jail!"

"So you were, my dear," said the man. He was a very fat man with a tremendous shock of white hair. "Now let us introduce ourselves," he went on, extending his hand, "my name is Pete Uspy."

"My name is Candy Christian," said the girl, "how do you do?"

"Glad to be acquainted with you," said Pete Uspy. He had a sort of Russian accent. "Yes, you were going to the jail all right, that much is certain. Now we've got to get you out of this town. Tonight."

"Out of town?" said Candy, "Good Grief, what have *I* done?"

"Ho," said Pete Uspy, putting one hand to his great brow, "who can say? All of that is mere mirage anyway. The point is this, that these authorities, whoever they were, policemen or whatever you wish to call them—is only a name—have the *material* viewpoint only and so would have put you physically in the jail. That much is certain."

There was something in Pete Uspy's manner which reminded Candy of Professor Mephesto, despite the former's atrocious accent, and she felt a confidence and rapport warming inside her.

"Yes, they certainly weren't very *spiritual*," she agreed.

"Certainly not," said Pete Uspy. "They had no spiritual advancement whatever!"

"*I'll* say," said Candy. She began trying to smooth out her skirt, which was wrinkled and still quite wet. "Ugh, these things are all icky," she said. "I don't know whether to keep them on or not!"

"No matter," said Pete Uspy, "is mere appearance. We are almost to the Foundation."

The cab pulled up in front of a large brownstone on 73rd Street and stopped.

"Here you are," said the driver.

"Good," said Peter Uspy, "here is the Foundation. Come, we must go inside it."

He got out and paid the driver and helped Candy out.

"Good Night, I hate to go in like this," she said, "I must look a sight."

"No, is very good," said Pete Uspy, "is material pathos. The Crackers are fond of this. Come."

He led the way up the steps and into a large foyer. A receptionist was there and he went directly to her.

"This girl is in need," he said, "and she wishes to help others. Have you material work for her?"

"Well," said the receptionist, "we have that crew in Minnesota. They could certainly use help out there."

"Just what I was thinking," said Pete Uspy. "She must go at once. Tonight." He seemed to have a strange hypnotic power over the receptionist.

"Yes, of course," she said, looking into his eyes. 'I will arrange for the transportation."

"Good," said Pete Uspy, "we will wait here." And he led Candy to an alcove in the foyer, where several chairs and a table were placed.

"Are you familiar with the Cracker work?" he asked when they were seated.

"Oh yes, of course," she said, "they're pacifists. . . . I know that much anyway."

"Ah yes, they are pacifists, but also they do much work in helping others. They have fine spiritual advancement, and you will find great camaraderie among them. It will be much fun for you."

"Yes, I *am* interested in their work," said Candy, "but I don't see how I can go there *now*. I mean, Good Grief, what about my apartment and all my things?" She was thinking too now of Derek.

"You *must* go," said Pete Uspy, "it is the only means of escaping the physical jail. Then when this affair has blown over, you will come back. Only a few days perhaps. Give me the keys to your apartment. I will see to it."

"I don't know," said the girl reluctantly, "I should at least go by there and pack some things." She felt her sopping skirt again. "These things are so icky, you have no idea."

"The Cracker people will give you something dry to wear," Pete Uspy promised. "A simple cloth shift."

"I like simple clothes," Candy admitted, nodding.

"Yes, clothes do not matter; it is folly to judge the pork chop by its wrapper."

"Is that a Cracker saying?" Candy asked.

"No, that is a Chinese proverb—I have taken it from the book of the *I. Ching*."

"I love the Chinese," said Candy, "I think they are the most spiritually advanced of all people—the man in the street, I mean to say."

"The Chinese-man in the street!" said Pete Uspy, chuckling. "Very good."

"Chinese *cooking* is very good, isn't it?" said Candy. "I can make several Chinese dishes." She wanted to name some of them for him and perhaps arrange for him to have dinner with her and Derek, but Pete Uspy said:

"Now, we have little time. The car will be here in a moment to take you to the airport. They will tell you what to do and, in fact, someone will be at the plane to meet you in Minnesota. When you get to the camp, you will find a friend of mine there among the common workers—he will help you. His wisdom is infinite and he is the greatest spiritual teacher of our times."

"Good Gosh," said Candy, "you mean I really must go? *Tonight?*"

"Oh yes, that much is certain—you cannot risk going to jail. It would greatly damage your spiritual advancement. For me it does not matter, I see through the mirage. But for you, a beautiful sensitive girl, it would be terrible. They would do terrible things to you, undress you and everything."

"Good Heavens!"

"Yes, so you see we must fight fire *with* fire. They wish to confine you in physical form, we will *escape* in that form!"

"Gosh," said Candy, "I don't know what to say."

"He who *knows* need not speak; he who *speaks* does not know," said Pete Uspy, . . . "give me the keys."

Candy fished them uncertainly out of her bag. She was wondering if she shouldn't tell him about Derek, and leave a message of some sort; but then she decided she would write a letter of explanation as soon as she reached the Cracker camp.

"The small one is the mailbox key," said the girl, handing them over. "I'll be writing to someone there . . . a friend of mine. Will you give him the letter when he comes to see me? His name is Derek."

"Of course," said Pete Uspy, "that shall be as you wish. Now we must get you a dry shift."

He got up and went again to the receptionist's desk, where he spoke briefly to the attentive woman. Then he returned to Candy.

"Good," he said, "she will give you dry."

"Oh that's wonderful," said Candy.

Pete Uspy remained standing.

"Now I must go," he said. "I have much work before me this night."

"How will I know your friend at the camp?" the girl asked anxiously.

"Ho," said Pete Uspy, "you will know him—*he* will know you, that much is certain. Do not worry, I will contact him that you are coming."

"Well," said Candy, standing and shaking hands, "thanks for everything."

Pete Uspy shrugged.

"Is nothing," he said, "is mere appearance."

"Well, you *did* save me from the jail and all those other things," Candy insisted.

"That is my pleasure," said Pete Uspy. "Now I say good night to you. Write to me before you return."

"Oh yes, I will," said Candy, "I'll write as soon as I get there!"

"Good," said Pete Uspy, turning to go. "Good night, and *bon voyage!*"

"Good night," said Candy, feeling again that tinge of wistful regret she always felt when she parted with anyone. She stood for a moment looking after him, before she was aware that the receptionist was trying to get her attention from the desk. She went over.

"Here is something dry and serviceable for you to wear," said the receptionist, handing the girl a folded garment. "You can change in the dressing room behind that alcove." She indicated with a nod a small door nearby.

"Thank you very much," said Candy cheerfully, and she crossed over to the dressing-room door and went inside. She began to feel a growing excitement about her work with the Cracker group. Inside the dressing room, she slipped off her skirt and panties.

"These prissy little panties are still wet!" she said, squeezing them into a tiny ball and giving them a kiss. Then she took off her sweater and brassiere and put on the simple garment, a sort of formless sackcloth shift with three buttons at the top. There was a mirror in the dressing room and she studied her appearance in it. She loved the simple garment. It must have been such a garb as this, she reflected, that Joan of Arc had worn to her execution. She began to feel quite like a saint. Wrapping her other clothes in a bundle, she went into the foyer again and to the receptionist's desk, presenting herself there as though to be inspected.

"It looks very nice," said the receptionist, perhaps slightly more interested than she should have been.

Candy did a little pirouette of joy, twirling the skirt just above her sweet knees.

"Oh, I feel younger than I have for years!" she cried. "And alive, really alive for the first time in my life!"

She handed the bundle of clothes to the receptionist.

"Here," she said, "I *won't* be needing *these!* Give them to someone . . . to some very *old* person, to someone still living in the Stone Age!"

She was ecstatically happy in her new garb. It was made of a heavy sort of canvas sackcloth, shaped somewhat like an inverted funnel, and came almost to her ankles.

"Now tell me *all* about the Crackers!" she gaily demanded.

"Well," said the receptionist, "I'm afraid there isn't time for *me* to tell you, I see your transportation to the airport has just arrived out front. But here . . ." She took some booklets and folders out of her desk and gave them to Candy. "You can browse through these on the plane."

"Oh wonderful!" said the girl, glancing through them. She was going to read a bit aloud, but the receptionist took her up again:

"I think you'd better go now," she said, "so you'll be in good time for your plane."

"All right," said Candy with real cheer, "thanks so much for everything, for having me, and . . . for *everything!*"

She leaned forward and kissed the receptionist.

"Good-bye," said the receptionist, "and good luck!"

"Good-bye," said Candy, running a few steps, and turning to wave, "good-bye, good-bye!"

Then she hurried on, calling out ahead of her to the car in front of the Foundation:

"Wait for me! Here I come!"

thirteen

13

On the plane, Candy settled herself comfortably, and thought about the events of the day. It had been a full day for her, and a tiring one; now she was glad to relax. She was impressed by Pete Uspy; his great head and quiet voice were with her still. He had seemed so self-sufficient, and Candy felt that he contained some secret and unspoken power. She wondered if she were falling in love with him, and she quickly turned her thoughts to Derek. No, she would not betray Derek, she *could not* betray him.

She got out the booklets and various literature the receptionist had given her and began to leisurely leaf through them. She suddenly found herself very tired though, deliciously drowsy, and so she let her lovely big eyes close in rest. She dropped into a light sleep almost at once, and began to dream:

She dreamed that she and her father were together in a great wide field of wild flowers on a beautiful summery day. He was lying there reciting poems of Mallarmé, but it was as if he himself had written them; and Candy was much younger, and she ran about the fields picking flowers, and though she would sometimes be at quite a distance from her father, she could hear every line he spoke. He spoke the lines perfectly, with exactly the right intonation and feeling for each word. Sometimes when he finished a poem, he would say: "That wasn't a bad poem. Now here's another—this is one I wrote for *you*, sweetheart; it came to me in a *flash*—in a terrible, beautiful flash just as I was releasing the sweet powerful seed from my testis that made you!"

"Oh Daddy," she would cry peevishly, "it *isn't* for me— it's for some other little girl!" And she would feel very sad, and standing before him with her pretty head bowed she would hold her tiny bouquet of flowers down in such a way that everything seemed helpless and pathetic. Then as she slowly raised her head and a big golden tear began to tumble down her cheek, she would say: "It's for *Mommy!*"

"Oh you silly sweetheart!" Daddy would cry gaily, holding his arms out to her. "It's for *you!* For you alone! You're my mommy and my sweetheart and my little darling girl!" And she would fly to his arms and nestle there while he began stroking her hair, her neck, her shoulders . . . and then she awoke, feeling cool and refreshed for the first time in her life, she thought, but blushing a little when she recalled the part about "the sweet powerful seed of my testis." It was true poetry, and she wished so much that she could share it with Daddy. Perhaps she could call him from the Cracker camp; but no, of course he would never understand, not in a million years, especially not in his present condition. But she *could* tell Derek; he would understand, and her heart warmed and throbbed with the idea. She mustn't forget it, she told herself.

When the big plane touched down at Mohawk, Minnesota, a few minutes after nine, Candy straightened her shift, saw to her facial appearance—she had removed all her makeup, but her lips were naturally as red and full as a great crimson gash—and flounced her lovely ringlets a few times before leaving her seat.

To her joy, there was a jeep to meet her at the edge of the simple airstrip. It was clearly marked along its side: CRACKER, and there were several young people in it already, who dismounted and came genially forward to welcome her. They introduced themselves and helped her into the jeep. "Well, let's don't sit here yakking," said one of them, "I'll bet this Cracker could use some chow!" "I'll say!" said Candy, quick to take hold of their exuberant spirit. And they were off like the wind, flying along the dark country roads outside Mohawk. The top of the jeep was down, and it was a lovely moonlit night. Soon they were singing, joyfully, at the top of their voices:

> "We are the Crackers, the Crackers are we!
> True to each Cracker as Crackers can be!
> We've got to build, boys and girls,
>   for a world of peace!

> A world of peace, a world of peace,
>   without silly police!
>   without silly police!

QUACK–QUACK! CRACKER!
QUACK–QUACK! CRACKER!"

It was a rousing tune, and Candy was quick to join in the merriment—rocking her body back and forth in unison with the others, and singing happily. These kids were lots of fun, she decided.

Mohawk is a coal-mining region and they passed a number of small mining towns en route to the camp, which was, as it turned out, situated just on the edge of one of these small villages—for that was the nature of the project which Candy had joined: to help with mining. The mines were shorthanded at this particular moment, and just when the country most needed its every ounce of coal to step up steel production and get cracking on the clean-fallout missile program.

The camp consisted of two large tents with many-tiered bunks; one tent for boys, the other for girls. Besides those, there were two small tents: the chow-tent and the rec-tent, the latter containing simply a Ping-Pong table and half a dozen paperback books.

Candy was shown directly to her bunk after being welcomed by those who had not been at the airport to meet her.

"This is where you're bunking down," said a friendly but impassive girl with dark hair which came to her waist, as she showed Candy the place. "The head," by which she meant the toilet, "is just over there," and she pointed to a little bucket behind a screen in the corner. "Stow your gear, and we'll get some hot chow into you."

"Roger!" said Candy, and a minute later she and the

dark-haired girl left the dormitory-tent and crossed over to the chow-tent nearby.

"This trooper could use some chow," said the dark-haired girl to the jolly fat cook who was there.

"Roger-dodger!" said the cook and ladled out a nice bowl of hot broth for Candy.

"Oh wonderful!" said Candy, holding the bowl in both hands and drinking it, allowing just her big lovely eyes to show above the rim. "Broth and porridge are my favorite dishes."

"Mine too," agreed the dark-haired girl.

After the simple meal, Candy felt refreshed and ready for her Cracker work to begin. Although it was about ten o'clock, some of the shafts were still open and it was agreed that she could go down into "No. 9" and work for a while that night if she wished. She was all too keen for it.

"You can have some coveralls if you want," said the dark-haired girl, "though most of us like to work in our regular clothes, and then keep them on—it gives us a real sense of the work we're doing, and isn't so hypocritical as changing."

Candy saw now that the girl's clothes were quite black from coal-dust, as were her hair and face.

"That's for me!" said Candy.

She was taken to the elevator of the shaft by the dark-haired girl, who said:

"Now, when you get down to the *third* level, you get off and walk straight ahead of you till you come to the end of the shaft. You can dig there for a while, it's lots of fun. It's about a mile to the end."

"Wonderful," said Candy. "Will anyone else be there?"

"Yes, I think so," said the dark-haired girl, then added with a frown: "Unless they're goofing off. We've had a lot of goofing off lately—especially among the *boys*."

"They'd better get on the *ball!*" said Candy, cross at the thought of these boys goofing off.

"I'll say," said the dark-haired girl, "it isn't funny! All *they* care about is getting into your pants—and then they're too tired to help with the mining. A pretty girl has to be *very* careful with boys."

"You're telling me!" said Candy. "And how!"

They would have liked to stay together and talk some more, but the elevator had reached the top of the entrance.

"You'd better go on now," said the dark-haired girl, "it takes about an hour to get to the bottom. We can talk some more when you get back. By the way, you'll find a little green-handled pick there. That's the one I always use."

"Roger," said Candy. She wished she could salute, but thought it would be silly since everything was so informal. She got into the elevator and pressed the button marked 3RD LEVEL, and was on her way down, waving back up at the dark-haired girl who watched the rapid descent from above.

Down, down went the little platform Candy was standing on, down, down and it was soon flying through absolute blackness. It was plenty exciting for the young girl and made her dear young tummy tingle.

Finally the elevator reached the third level, and Candy got off and started walking. The shaft was quite dark, but from one bend to another she could always just make out the faint glow of light ahead. At last she came to a long, unbroken stretch of shaft and she could see the soft light

glowing at the end. As she got nearer, she could also make
out the figure of a man there. He was sitting on a camp
stool reading a paperback novel by the lamp overhead.

When Candy reached him he acknowledged her with a
nod.

"Hi," said Candy, a bit breathless but more keen for her
work to begin. She looked around for the little green-
handled pick that the dark-haired girl had told her about,
found it, and started hacking at the wall of coal.

The man watched her curiously.

"So, you have come," he said at last.

Candy wondered why he wasn't helping with the work
instead of sitting there reading, and she decided that he
might be one of the boys the dark-haired girl had com-
plained about.

"Yes, and *we'd* better get cracking on this work!" she
said without looking at him.

The man nodded.

"I have been expecting you," he said.

There was something in his odd tone that caused Candy
to turn and look at him now for the first time. He wasn't
a boy at all she saw then, but a man of . . . though as she
scrutinized his face for a clue to age she felt she had never
seen anyone whose age was so indeterminate. Anyway, she
thought, with an urgent flutter somewhere behind her
precious labia, he was not a boy but a *man*. Large, with a
great bald head, and huge black mustache, his eyes blazed
at her in the half-light; and if Pete Uspy had been impressive with his strange eyes, this man was a veritable Svengali.
She knew at once that he was the man Pete Uspy had

spoken of, and she knew too somehow that he was to be very important in her life.

"Are you . . ." she faltered.

"*I,*" he said with soft drama, "am . . . *Grindle.*"

Candy was confused and embarrassed by his piercing look, which seemed to her to be undoing the top buttons of her shift and moving across her bare breast where the nipples now began slowly distending and throbbed painfully. She turned her eyes back to the wall and hacked at it some more, and the man looked down at his novel again. Candy was sure that he was the most spiritually advanced person she had met and she wondered what she should say to him. She tried to lose herself for the moment in her work and began a furious peck and flurry with the little pick. From time to time she would stop to get her breath and to scoop the chips she had done into a tiny pile. About the fourth time she stopped to do this, the man on the camp-stool raised his eyes from the book.

"That is enough chopping the coal," he said. His accent, like Pete Uspy's, was very strong, though not at all unpleasant. In fact it seemed to add a certain poetic seriousness and drama to his words. Candy had no doubt that he was in charge of this section of the mine, so she was quite ready to obey; also she was tired of the work now. "Roger," she said, and gathered her remaining chips into the little pile she had begun.

"Your work is well," said the big man watching her.

"Thanks," said Candy, brushing her hands; she felt the warm sustaining glow of accomplishment within her. "We could use some chow after *that* work," she said.

The big man put the novel in his pocket.

"I do not care to eat," he said, standing up. "However, let us leave this mine now."

"Right," said Candy, ". . . but what about the coal?" She was looking at the pile she had dug.

"Yes, you'd better bring that along. Here . . ." He took out his handkerchief and spread it on the ground so that Candy could scoop her coal onto it; then she tied it in a little bundle and held it up by her shoulder, but it was awkward there, so she put it in the pocket of her shift, and they started walking back to the elevator.

The big man beside her began absently humming the Cracker song, and Candy joined in. This seemed to bring him out of his reverie.

"I'm sorry," he said, "I didn't realize I was humming that song. As a matter of fact I don't like to hear it. Not for the moment anyway. I hope you understand."

"Yes, of course," said the girl. She was confused by this, yet it was not wholly an unpleasant sensation.

Soon enough, considering the distance, they were at the elevator shaft once more and got in it.

"I will operate the machine," said the big man. It was the first thing he had said since objecting to the song about a mile back, and after scrutinizing the buttons for a moment, he pressed the top one, marked GROUND LEVEL.

The elevator started rising.

"Good," said the big man. "Up we go. Up, up, up!"

It seemed to Candy that he was in a jovial mood now, and she decided to risk a question.

"Did Mr. Uspy write to you about me?" she asked, not realizing for the moment that of course there had hardly been time for a letter.

The big man looked at her a few seconds without speaking. Then he said: "I am in telepathic communication with Mr. Uspy, from time to time during the night and day. I knew that you were coming. Yes. *And* that you have good spiritual advancement."

"Gosh," said Candy, "he said *that?*"

"I know that it is so—you have come, seeking truth, have you not?"

"Oh yes," the girl was quick to assure him.

"Then you have come to the right place—we will begin at once. Tonight."

The attention of the great man, denied her up to this moment, was now like a luxurious bath to the young girl.

"I . . . I hardly know what to say," she began with gratitude.

"He who knows need not speak; he who speaks does not know."

"That's what Mr. Uspy says!" cried Candy with the delight she always derived from knowledge.

"He got that from me," said the big man. "He is my secretary."

He stated it factually, as a child would, without pride or embarrassment; but it was a fact quite impressive to Candy even so, because of her strong memory of Mr. Uspy and the day behind her, so much of which was connected with Derek and the warmth of her own joyous heart.

fourteen

14

In the rec-tent, after a cup of hot chocolate, Candy and great Grindle sat talking—he on the edge of the Ping-Pong table, and she at his feet.

"What stage of spiritual advancement are you in at present?" he asked the girl.

"Gosh, I have no idea," she said.

"Ah yes, the heart knows," he said. "And the heart knows best."

"I think I'm in an early stage of some sort," said the girl with perfect candor.

"There are six stages along the mystic path," said great Grindle, "and you are in one of them or another, at all times. Now your *first* stage is this: to have read a large number of books on the various religions and philosophies, and to have listened to many learned doctors profess the different doctrines—and then to experiment seriously yourself with a number of doctrines."

"That's only the *first* stage?" asked Candy, hardly able to believe it.

"Yes. The path is arduous, you see—many take it; few arrive."

"What is the second stage?"

"The second stage is to choose one doctrine from among the many one has studied and discard the others—just as the eagle carries off only one sheep from the flock."

"Gosh," said Candy.

"Then does the path become truly arduous. The third stage is to remain in a lowly condition, humble in one's demeanor, not seeking to be conspicuous or important in the eyes of the world—but behind apparent insignificance, to let one's mind soar above all worldly power and glory."

"And then?"

"Then you must attain the fourth stage: *indifference to all*. Behaving like the dog or the pig which eats what chance brings it. Not making any choice among the things one meets. Abstaining from effort to acquire or avoid things. Accepting with equal indifference whatever comes: riches or poverty, praise or contempt. Giving up the distinction between virtue and vice, honorable and shameful, good and evil . . . neither repenting nor rejoicing over what one may have done in the past."

Candy was enjoying it immensely. She settled herself more comfortably.

"Then what?" she asked, wide-eyed and lovely.

"Then do you attain to your *fifth* stage," said great Grindle, "there to consider with perfect equanimity and detachment the conflicting opinions and the various manifestations of the activity of beings. To understand that such is the nature of things, the inevitable mode of action of each . . . and to remain always *serene*. To look at the world as a man standing on the highest mountain of the country looks at the valleys and lesser summits spread out below him. That is your fifth stage."

"Good Grief," said Candy.

"Yes, the mystic path is an arduous path, you see; many depart, few arrive."

"What on earth is the sixth stage?" the girl wanted to know.

"The sixth stage cannot be described in words, unfortunately. It corresponds to the realization of the *void*, which, in Lamaist terminology, means the Inexpressible Reality."

"I don't get it," said Candy.

"Well," said great Grindle, "one must understand here the realization of the non-existence of a permanent *ego*. This is your great Tibetan formula: 'The person is devoid of self; all things are devoid of self.' "

"And that's the end?" said Candy after a moment.

"Yes, for all practical purposes it is. There *is* a seventh stage, physically, of *suspended animation*. But that need not concern us here."

"Suspended animation!" cried Candy, as though that pleased her more than the rest.

Great Grindle nodded, and the girl gave him a searching look, wondering indeed if he were not capable of this feat himself.

"Gosh, I'd *love* to be able to do that," she admitted at last.

"The path is arduous," said Grindle.

"And how!" said Candy.

"Well, what do you say? Will you walk the mystic path? Already you have good spiritual advancement."

"Well, I *would* like to try," she said, "what do we do first?"

"First you must have a good *guru,* a spiritual teacher, to train you."

"And you . . ." Candy began.

"I shall be your *guru.*"

"Oh that's wonderful," said the girl; she was doubly pleased and stood up as though to kiss great Grindle; but he was quick to reassert a more formal tone.

"First," he said, "there is the problem of mental discipline and the basic yoga exercises."

He drew out a bead necklace from his pocket, not unlike a rosary chain, with the beads arranged along it in varying groups, and he placed this around Candy's neck, the girl arching her slender throat graciously to receive it. Then he explained how she was to practice her yoga breathing patterns by feeling the different groupings of beads along the necklace.

Next came instruction in the famous exercise of "opposing thumbs," then the secret of "standing sleep," whereby the successful practitioner can receive the physical benefit of 14 hours' uninterrupted sleep in only two or three minutes while standing with his head pressing firmly into a stone which he has placed against the wall.

"Now, perhaps your most important yoga exercise," said great Grindle, with extreme seriousness, "is your Exercise Number Four, for it is the true key to Infinite Oneness— I speak, of course, of the *Cosmic Rhythm,* which you must achieve to be in harmony with all things, and to find Nirvana. Now, relax your body, and let it follow movements which the pressure of my hands on it suggests."

So saying, he placed his hands on Candy's slim, rounded hips and began to rotate them slowly, back and forth, in a smooth undulating motion.

"Just so," he said, stepping back to watch her performance, "yes, very good."

The movement, in any other than a mystical context, would have seemed suggestively sexual, and perhaps even obscene; Candy was aware of this and her lovely face went crimson for an instant, but she crossly blamed herself for making the association and attributed it to her own impure and undeveloped spirit.

While she was practicing Exercise Number Four, and Grindle was directing her, causing her by command to vary the tempo of her gyrations, the dark-haired girl, who had suggested the little green-handled pick to Candy earlier, appeared in the tent doorway and stood watching for a moment, at no pains to conceal the disapproval she felt.

"*Very pretty,*" she said, after a moment, and with stinging bitterness.

Candy, so intent on mastering the exercise, had not noticed the girl's arrival, and was slightly taken aback by the sudden sound of her voice, as indeed was great Grindle himself, completely absorbed in seeing that the execution was correct. At the girl's words, he gave a bellow of rage, wheeled and rushed against her with clenched fists, as she, in turn, fled hurriedly from the tent.

"He pretends he's a weirdie," she cried in retreat, "but

he's just trying to get into your little sugar-scoop!" But her voice trailed away, almost unheard in the darkness beyond the tent.

"That cheap Philistine!" said Grindle in genuine annoyance as he came back to Candy. "What she needs is a horsewhipping!"

Candy was impressed by his show of heat and impatience at the interruption, and was pleasingly flattered that he had such an interest in her progress with the exercises. Certainly too she was keen to get on with her mastery of them and to achieve some real advancement along the mystical path. She tried to divert his annoyance by doubling her zeal in practicing.

"Yes!" said Grindle. "Excellent! Now then, our next . . ." But he stopped short and put his great head sideways in an attitude of listening.

"Hark!" he said.

Then Candy heard it too, a faint whistling, very near the rec-tent.

"Wait here," said Grindle as he got off the Ping-Pong table and went to the door of the tent. "That is your next exercise: wait here and think of nothing."

"Right!" said Candy.

Grindle went out the door into the night, and Candy tried to make her mind a blank, but she was too excited for the moment to do so. She thought if she went to the tent door and looked up into the dark sky, she would be able to do it. "*Unless* there are stars!" she said half aloud, and she walked to the tent door and looked out at the sky. As she did, however, she could not help but catch a glimpse of great Grindle, standing in the shadows, at the unloading ramp, standing near the same rail-cart into which she herself had earlier placed her small diggings of coal. He was talking in a low voice to two men there, and one of them seemed to be giving him something—*money*, it appeared to be, from the deliberate way he was handing it over, little by little, as though counting it out, and rather furtively too. Then the two men began quietly pushing the rail-cart down the track and away. Evidently Grindle had just sold a cart of the Cracker coal.

This realization came as a shock to Candy, and she drew away from the door and lowered her head to pout prettily, not raising it when Grindle reentered the tent seconds later. He was rubbing his hands together briskly—in a manner actually suggesting the accomplishment Candy knew of already, to her repulsion and horror.

"Well!" said Grindle with great gusto. "Now then! Where was I?"

"You *were*," said the girl with cutting hauteur, "at the point of selling a cartload of Cracker coal!" And she burst into tears, covering her face and rushing to one corner of the tent.

"How *could* you?" she cried, really brokenhearted. "How *could you?*"

Surprisingly, great Grindle did not seem taken aback by this accusation, but only slightly annoyed at her outburst, and the sound of her crying, which he seemed to find unpleasant.

"*That!*" he said, waving his hand and frowning with impatience. "That was nothing—a mere material transaction. Of no significance whatever."

"But why did you take the *money?*" the girl demanded,

raising her lovely tear-glittering face for a moment to show the hurt and betrayal she felt. "Mr. *Uspy* wouldn't have taken it!" she cried. *"He said it was all a dream, and so did you! He* wouldn't have taken it, and he's only your *secretary!* I think it's awful!" And she hid her face again, sobbing terribly.

"What did he say it was?" asked Grindle, coming near her.

"A dream!" whimpered the girl in a child's voice. "He said it was all a dream, and so did you!"

"Of course it is a dream," said Grindle, placing a hand on Candy's shoulder, *"all* reality . . ." his hand described an arc, searching for the word, ". . . is mere appearance, illusion. A *dream,* certainly."

"But why do you have to have money in a dream?" the girl wanted to know, tearful as ever.

"Ah!" said Grindle, his fingers toying the back of her sweet left ear, "it is a *dream,* yes—but we make it a pleasant dream, not a . . . a *cauchemar!"*

"But *you're* making it a *cauchemar* for the Crackers," said Candy, "selling their coal like that—it's . . . it's like *stealing!"* The last word, and the host of implications it held, caused her to sob anew, oblivious, it seemed, to the lavish caresses along her neck and spine, with which Grindle was trying to soothe her.

"Let me ask you this . . ." said Grindle, *"who* are the happiest people in our world? Who besides, of course, those well advanced on the mystical path are happiest? Is it not those who *create?* Of course! It is the *artist.* It is the artist who is self-sufficient and happiest in our world. Yes! But the great art comes from those who have *suffered*—

history will bear me out!" In his discourse, he had abandoned the girl for the moment and was pacing about the tent; this may have been what caused her now to raise her eyes like two saucers and stare after him, somewhat longingly it seemed.

"History will bear me out," he repeated, "it is the deprived cultures who have produced the greatest number of artists; thus have we, here tonight, struck a blow for all that is fine and good in the dream world! *Art!* The danger, of course, is that these Crackers are on the primary level of participation in the privation-experience, namely that of shoddy masochism! However, in any case it makes no difference." Candy was watching him wide-eyed and he returned to where she was standing in the corner of the tent. This had the effect of relieving her anxiety in one way, but made her renew her tears just the same.

"Oh, I don't know," she said, hiding her face, "it just seems so . . . so *shoddy,* taking the money like that."

"Shoddy!" said Grindle. "Twenty dollars I got for it . . . what's shoddy about that?" He took the bills out of his pocket and stared at them. "Look," he said, holding the money toward her.

"No, no," said Candy, shaking her head blindly.

"Very well," said Grindle, "then I shall . . . shall *eat* it." And he made an abrupt movement of his hand to his mouth, pretending to put the money in, though adroitly palming it instead.

"Oh no, don't!" cried Candy, raising her eyes and touching his arm in real concern.

"Too late! Too late!" said Grindle, chewing vigorously,

"I'm eating it! I'm eating it! Down it goes!" He pretended to swallow mightily. "There!" he said. "All gone!"

This left Candy with a tremendous feeling of responsibility for the loss.

"Oh, I don't know *what* to say," she cried, squeezing his arm.

"It doesn't matter," said Grindle, as he surreptitiously pocketed the loot; he lowered his head, looking almost sheepish. "It was just . . . just that I wanted to . . . to buy something pretty for you," he said, and he allowed a tear to form in his eye and to slowly course down his heavy jowl.

"*What?*" said the girl, too amazed. "Oh my darling," she said, putting her arms around him, "my precious baby," and she stroked and fondled him feverishly to bring comfort, drawing his great head down to her shoulder and rocking it there like a big strange infant.

They were standing like this then, with Grindle letting his massive head slide down the front of the girl's shift, cleverly manipulating his huge cleft chin to undo the buttons of it, when four or five young people came into the tent.

"Break it up, you Crackers!" said one of the boys jovially. "We're going to have a campfire sing! Come on, join the gang!" And they were soon gathered around the two, hustling them along outside for some group fun.

Round the blazing campfire, the young people's voices lifted in the rousing Cracker song:

"Quack! Quack! Quack!" they were shouting.

No sooner had Candy and Grindle, escorted by the

others, joined the group, than Grindle drew the girl aside into the shadows.

"More important work awaits us," he said, inadvertently, or so it seemed, touching her crotch for a moment. "Come."

So saying, he took her hand and led the way, along the rocky path and down the bramblebush hill to a stream there at the bottom, which they followed then, curving around the hill and the Cracker camp above.

Candy ran alongside the stream, lifting her skirt a bit, terribly excited by the wild moonlit aspect of the countryside and overjoyed at this sort of informal outing she and Grindle were having—so unlike anything she had ever done with Daddy.

Round a bend, and they came to a shimmering pool, and behind it a grotto, or water-cave, the mouth of it dark against the silver water.

"Oh, how lovely!" cried the girl, clasping her hands together at her breast, as though the sight were so lovely indeed that it gave her a pang there.

"Come," said Grindle, taking her hand again, "we must go inside."

They had to walk through a foot or so of water to reach the mouth of the grotto, which Candy did with little squeals and shrieks of pure delight: then they were inside, and Grindle lit a lamp that was sitting on the wide reef-ledge of the grotto. With this soft yellow light and the moon coming in through the mouth, the already interesting interior, its cavernous roof spidered with stalactite formations and glints of quartz, took on a quite remarkable beauty. Blue-green moss and richest fern grew in abundance along the walls and on the ledge itself, forming a veritable carpet there, the thickness, almost, of a love-couch.

"The path is arduous," Grindle intoned. "This is where I give lessons."

"Oh it's just too marvelous," said Candy in a whisper, looking down now into the blue pool itself and the deep, wavering splinters of phosphorus below the surface.

Grindle, though, was watching the young girl; in this setting she was nothing so much as a perfect nymph, or the immortal beauty Diana herself.

"It's good that you wear that simple shift," he said, matter-of-factly, "it will expedite the next lesson considerably."

"Are we really to have another mystical lesson now!" exclaimed Candy in sheer delight, actually giving a little jump of joy; it was all *too* perfect already! And now another mystical lesson as well! She sat down eagerly on the fluffy bed of moss, arranged her skirt primly, tucking it under her precious knees, getting comfortable and making her mind ready and alert, just the way she had always done in the interesting courses at school. She had a momentary regret that she didn't have her notebook and pencil along, but she quickly dismissed this thought for the infinitely more preferable notion of Arcadia, with the students sitting around under the trees, listening to the master talk, and *not* taking notes but absorbing everything, everything. That's the *pure* way and the *true way*, thought Candy and was extremely pleased.

"First," said Grindle, sitting down beside her, "we'll want to get out of this worldly apparel." And he began taking off his wet shoes. Then he started undoing his trousers.

"Do we *have* to?" asked the girl uneasily; she hadn't anticipated this and was somehow put off by the idea.

" 'Put your house in order,' " quoted Grindle, " 'that is the *first* step.' Certainly we must divest ourselves of all material concern—in both spirit and body."

"Right!" said Candy firmly, in an effort to dispel the great warm reservoir of feminine modesty she felt glowing up inside her and finally flushing her pretty face, as she slipped out of the simple garment.

"There!" she said pertly, and in an abrupt little movement that spoke well of her bravery, she put aside the simple shift, which was all she was wearing, and gave a little sigh of relief that she had actually been able to do it; and yet, even as she was sensing a certain pride and accomplishment in the feat, her sweet face flushed maidenly rose as, under Grindle's gaze, she felt her smart little nipples tauten and distend, as though they, alerted now, had a life quite their own.

"Good!" said Grindle. "Now then, lace your fingers together, in the yoga manner, and place them behind your head. Yes, just so. Now then, lie back on the mossy bed."

"Oh gosh," said Candy, feeling apprehensive, and as she obediently lay back, she raised one of her handsome thighs slightly, turning it inward, pressed against the other, in a charmingly coy effort to conceal her marvelous little spice-box.

"No, no," said Grindle, coming forward to make adjustments, "legs well apart."

At his touch, the darling girl started in fright and diffidence, but Grindle was quick to reassure her.

"I'm a doctor of the soul," he said coldly; "I am certainly not interested in that silly little body of yours—it is the *spirit* that concerns us here. Now is that understood?"

"Yes," answered the girl meekly, lying very still now and allowing him to adjust her limbs, just so, well apart, and turned out slightly.

"Eyes closed," said Grindle firmly, and when Candy had obeyed, he sat back and surveyed the whole.

"Good!" he said at last. "Now then. This lesson will be devoted to the transcendence of the bodily senses. Under my guidance you shall achieve the ability to master all bodily feeling. Is that clear?"

"Yes," whispered the closed-eyed girl. She was greatly reassured by Grindle's tone, which was like that of an instructor in logic, but she was still flushing and somewhat annoyed with the way her pert little nips kept pulsing and pouting. Those bad little smart alecks! she thought crossly to herself.

Great Grindle leaned forward with outstretched fingers and allowed them to play idly across the golden melon of the girl's budding tummy. She moved a bit and even gave a little nervous laugh.

"Now, now," said Grindle sharply, "you're not a child! Try to be serious! The mystic path is not an easy one— many take it, few arrive."

Under this admonishment the girl sobered quickly enough and tried to order her thoughts.

"Now this is a so-called 'erogenous zone,'" explained

Grindle, gingerly taking one of the perfect little nipples which did so seem to be begging for attention between his thumb and forefinger, turning it gently back and forth.

"*I'll* say," the girl agreed, squirming despite her efforts to be serious.

"Yes," said Grindle, nodding sagely, "and this too, of course," taking the other one now, giving it a series of fondling tweaks, while the girl stirred uneasily.

"Now then," said Grindle, abandoning the nipples for the moment, leaving them there, like two tiny heads, craning up eagerly, and allowing his hands to caress slowly down the wondrous arch of Candy's delightful body, down the sides, along the hips and over the inner thighs to converge in the golden down, beneath which the fabulous lamb-pit was sweetening itself.

"Oh gosh," the girl murmured, as Grindle carefully turned back the rose-petal labes and revealed, in all its tiny splendor, the magnificent little jewel, the pink pearl clit, shimmering, it seemed, in absurdly delicious readiness.

"This is *another* of these so-called 'erogenous zones,' " announced Grindle contemptuously, addressing the perfect thing with his finger, giving it several gentle flicks.

"*And how,*" Candy was quick to agree, fidgeting now in spite of her attempts at control.

Great Grindle applied himself to massaging the clit adroitly.

"Goodness . . ." said the girl in soft fretfulness, ". . . I didn't know it was going to be like *this*."

"Yes, you must master these feelings," said Grindle easily. "One who is not master of his feelings is not master of his house—he is like the reed, tossed on the waves of chance. Tell me, how does it feel now?"

The lovely girl's great eyelids were fluttering.

"Oh, it's all tingling and everything," she admitted despairingly.

"First," said Grindle, continuing the massage, "you will learn *transcendence* of the senses, and in that way will you soar above all sensory concern; next you will learn *control* of the senses, whereby you may come at will—instantaneous orgasm, untouched, at my command."

He stopped the massage and raised himself to his knees.

"Open your eyes," he said. "I will show you an example of such control. You will notice that I have caused my member to become stout and rigid—as though it were in the so-called state of 'erection.' "

It was true, as the girl saw soon enough—Grindle close at hand displaying his taut member, and she flushed terribly and averted her eyes.

"No, no," said Grindle, raising her demure chin with his hand, "do not allow vulgar sexual or material associations to bear upon the matter—it is a demonstration of perfect sensory control. I have merely willed the member to become stout and rigid. It resembles the so-called *erection*, does it not? In the sixth stage, one masters *all* such muscular control, even that which is most involuntary—thus can one, by the will of the advanced intellect, achieve what was theretofore a secret of nature. Regard how I have willed my member: no base or material desire is connected with it, yet it resembles the so-called sexual erection. Does it not?"

The sweet girl nodded shyly, scarcely able to look.

"Yes. Touch it," said Grindle, "you will see for your-self."

He took her hand and encouraged it forward, and she touched it lightly. Being able to regard it now, imperson-ally, not as an object of lust but as a demonstration of spiritual advancement, made it a thing of interest to the young girl and she examined it curiously, touching it here and there, still with a certain reserve because of her past fearful associations—which she knew though, to be sure, were her own fault.

"You can squeeze it if you like," prompted Grindle, ". . . yes, do."

Candy squeezed the swollen member interestedly in her delicate grasp, and what appeared to be a drop of semen formed on the end.

"There!" said Grindle, in a manner of triumph. "See that drop—that's an example of *glandular* mastery as well! It is extremely rare. The late Rama Krishna approximated it, but did not fully achieve it in the end. I have willed the intricate chemistry and secretion of the fluid."

"Gosh," said Candy, raising her beautiful eyes to the great man, her face radiant now in frank reverence.

"Now resume the basic yoga position," said Grindle, "and I will continue with the instruction."

Candy lay back again with a sigh, closed-eyed, hands joined behind her head, and Grindle resumed his fondling of her sweet-dripping little fur-pie.

"Does the tingling sensation you referred to before con-tinue and increase?" he asked after a moment or so.

". . . I'm afraid so," said the girl sadly, panting a little.

"And do you experience feelings of creamy warmth and a great yielding sensation?" demanded Grindle.

"Yes," Candy sighed, thinking he was surely psychic.

"Now I'm going to put this member into you," said Grindle judiciously, "and in that way can the sensation of the so-called 'sexual act' be approximated and surveyed to advantage."

"Oh gosh," said Candy in real disquiet, unable, despite her efforts, to shake off all the old associations it had for her, ". . . do we really *have* to?" And, almost in reflex, she drew her marvelous thighs a bit closer together.

"Never mind your crass and absurdly cheap philistine materialist associations with it," said Grindle crossly, as he adjusted her legs again and ranged himself just above her. "Put those from your mind—concentrate on your *Exercise Number Four,* for always remember that we must bring *all* our mystical knowledge to converge on the issue at hand— even as does the tiger his strength, cunning, and speed."

"Now I am inserting the member," he explained, as he parted the tender quavering lips of the pink honeypot and allowed his stout member to be drawn slowly into the seething thermal pudding of the darling girl.

"Oh my goodness," said Candy, squirming her lithe and supple body slightly, though remaining obediently closed-eyed and with her hands clasped tightly behind her head.

"Now I shall remove the member," said Grindle, ". . . not all the way, but just so, there, and in again. You see? And again so, I will repeat this, several times—while you do your Exercise Number Four."

"Gosh," said Candy, swallowing nervously, ". . . I don't think I can concentrate on it now."

"Oh yes," said Grindle, encouraging her hips with his hands, setting them into the motion of the Cosmic Rhythm Exercise she had practiced earlier in the rec-tent. And when she had satisfactorily achieved the motion, Grindle said: "Now this, you see, approximates the so-called 'sexual act.' "

"I *know* it," said Candy fretfully, greatly distracted by the thought.

"I shall presently demonstrate still another mastery of glandular functions," claimed great Grindle, "that of the so-called *orgasm,* or *ejaculation.*"

"Oh please," said the adorable girl, actually alarmed, "not . . . not *inside* me . . . I . . . I . . ."

"Don't be absurd," said Grindle, breathing heavily, "naturally, in willing the chemistry of the semen, I would eliminate the impregnating agent, spermatozoa, as a constituent—for it would be of no use to our purposes here you see."

"Now then," he continued after a moment, "tell me if this does not almost exactly resemble the philistine 'orgasm'?"

". . . Oh gosh," murmured the darling closed-eyed girl, biting her lip as the burning member began to throb and spurt inside her, in a hot, ravaging flood of her precious little honey-cloister whose bleating pink-sugar walls cloyed and writhed as though alive with a thousand tiny insatiable tongues, ". . . *and how!*"

fifteen

15

During the next few days, in the course of instruction, it
was necessary for great Grindle to enter the adorable girl
with his member any number of times. It was decided, too,
that because of her need for periods of uninterrupted
meditation, it would be best for Candy to remain permanently in the grotto, rather than return to the camp.
Grindle would visit her there from time to time, bringing
food, checking her progress, and carrying on with the instruction.

On the sixth day though, the girl seemed apprehensive
when Grindle arrived.

"Are you *really* sure," she asked, wide-eyed and darling,
"that you willed out *all* the . . . the spermatozoa from
the semen?"

"Certainly," said Grindle with a show of impatience,
"why do you ask?"

"*Because,*" said Candy, lowering her voice and blushing

deeply, "my . . . my *period* is late. And it simply *never* is!"

"Ach," said Grindle, with a grimace of distaste to reassure her, *"nothing!* That is *nothing*—in fact, it is a good sign of spiritual advancement. You have transcended the need of it, you see. You have willed it away."

"Oh but I *wouldn't,*" said the girl, most convincingly, "I'm *terribly* worried when it's late!"

"Well, we shall see," said great Grindle.

The next day when he arrived he handed her an airplane ticket for Tibet.

"Yes," he said, "your spiritual advancement now is such that you are prepared for the highest enlightenment. You shall walk with the lamas of the holy East."

"Gosh," said Candy, so awed by the idea that she forgot for the moment her earlier worry—though then was quick to remember.

"But Good Grief—what about my *period?*"

"That is of no concern," said Grindle, with a frown of annoyance. "Spritually advanced people do not become, how do you say, 'pregnant.' Besides, what does it matter? It is merely a philistine concern."

"Well . . ." began the sweet girl uncertainly.

"Think no more of it whatsoever," said Grindle, "your thoughts should be on a much higher level. You are about to walk with the holy of the holy—such thoughts would shame their very shadows."

He glanced at his watch.

"Your plane is at 7:30—I believe we have time for one or two more exercises before your departure."

"Oh gosh," sighed Candy in resignation, getting into her

basic yoga position: it was certainly no joke, this mystical business, and far from being the easiest of paths for a young impressionable girl.

Forty-eight hours later Candy was standing in the mail line at the American Express in Calcutta.

"Anything for Candy Christian?" she asked brightly, and beamed when the dark-skinned clerk handed her two letters, one postmarked NEW YORK CITY, the other RACINE, WISCONSIN.

She went into the lounge, and after getting a cold Coke from the dispenser, took one of the green leatherette easy chairs near the window overlooking colorful Zen Boulevard and settled comfortably to read her mail from home.

She was sure the New York letter was from Derek, so she decided to save it till last, and she opened the other one, a delightfully scented lavender envelope addressed in the fashionable backhand of her Aunt Livia. It read:

Gittin' any? Hee-hee. You know I used to travel quite a bit myself. Yes, indeed; when I was in Italy! *Brother! I had so much of that hot greaser dago cock that I stopped* menstruating *and started* minestroning!

Well, if you can be serious for a second (which I doubt—*not with* your *little clit thumping away a mile-a-minute!) I'd just like to tell you that your fuddy-duddy old daddykins is missing in action! That's right, kiddo, he took it on the lam, split the scent, cut on out! Where, who knows?* "Cherchez la tight-pussy femme," *as Colette used to say. Anyway, due to an absurd "mix-up," it was your Uncle Jack who was there in the bed during our last bit of funfare at the old hôpital. Natch I was hip to the lay the moment I dug his joint—you may recall I conked on it, only to come up an hour later with an ass full of needles at the hands of Doktor J. O. Heeby-Jeeby himself! Well, you can bet your hot little tushy that he didn't get off easy! He had exposed himself, and I dug the de-frocked ding-dong of his (which I've no doubt you know only too well!) and shouted: "Stripped for action, eh Doc? Then let 'er rip!" He was all right—a bit self-conscious though to my way of thinking. Kept wanting to "jay-o" too. But then when it was in the goodie he changed his tune quickly enough and no mistake! I put those puppy-dog tongues on him and he said: "Good Christ! Good Christ!" Then I hit him with my snapping-turtle just as he was getting his big soulful Hebe nuts off and he yelled at the top of his voice: "CHRIST WAS A JEW!" Flipped him completely, you dig? I felt pretty good about it myself—I mean, me being thirty-four, and him a young soulful-looking cat, snapping his wig like that on account of my tight slick goodie—know what I mean? No, I don't suppose you would. Well then let me just tell you that if a woman don't function, she ain't shit. Think it over, kiddo.*

Anyway, I just wanted to put you in the general picture here in Racine. Do let us hear from you, Can-baby—all the best, and don't take any wooden organ!

AUNT LIVIA

With the letter's early reference to "menstruating," Candy had been sharply reminded of her own problem in this regard and hardly took in the rest, skimming it with disapproval because of some of the questionable phrases. She put the letter away and had a few sips of Coke before opening the other. It read:

Caught up in the sickening coil-spin of this lewd city—the waiting in bistros, the feigning, the crooked smile and the cold

gray winter of sodden remorse, the bone-dry jacked-off empti-
ness of everything—hardly the trappings for a frothy letter of
affectionate concern . . . and yet, with a nightmare grimace
of hilarity frozen onto my heartbreak, do I take pen to hand
and say how very much *I would like to have some of your*
snapping-turtle puss.

A FRIEND

Candy read and reread the letter. Was it from Derek?
Parts of it, of course, were pure poetry, and Candy wondered if it hadn't after all been written by Jack Katt or
Tom Smart, perhaps the only persons in the Village capable
of real poetry. And yet, it may have been automatic-writing
or stream-of-consciousness from Derek! She was terribly excited at the idea, and finished her Coke in two gulps. Then
she got up and went downstairs and out onto the boulevard.
She had just begun walking along when she felt a sudden
damp warmth down inside her little honey-pouch, and she
knew her dear period had finally come! "Thank Goodness!"
she said, and looked at once for a drugstore where she could
get some junior Tampons. She finally spotted an herb shop
and went in. The ancient native keeper was squatting on
the floor smoking hemp and could not understand her at
all. Candy, the shy precious, would not make the necessary
gestures to convey her meaning, so at last had to leave and
go back to the American Express, where she borrowed a
Tampon from one of the secretaries. It was not a junior-
size but a regular, and the adorable girl fretted about
whether or not it would go in—but she did finally manage
somehow, and then, happy and secure, she was off to the
great temple at the end of Zen Boulevard.

On the way she passed the ageless "holy man" who had been pointed out to her already as being one of the most advanced of India's mystics—an ash- and dung-covered old man wearing a simple loincloth, he seemed in a state of complete oblivion as he inched his way forward. Evidently, he was going to the temple too. A number of American tourists were following him along, taking pictures of him, trying to get him to pose, smile, or react in some way by offering him money and bits of bread. He seemed quite unaware of their presence however, shuffling along like a man in a trance, and when a cute little girl of six was sent up to him by one of the mothers to get his autograph, he appeared not even to see her. This caused a certain amount of bitter feeling in the crowd of tourists.

"Well, I think *that's* taking it too far," one woman was heard to say with indignation, "to just *ignore* that cute little child like that! 'Holy' or not, that's just plain *not nice!*"

"Hole-in-the-head is more like it if my guess is any good!" said the little girl's father, trying to comfort the child now. "It's all right, Doreen, he's just not a nice man!"

It made Candy furious to see these tourists wandering around, gawking at the temples and the holy men.

"They advertise that they want tourists," one of the men was saying, "they tell you you'll be welcome in their country—then we come over here, pour plenty of good dollars into the economy, and what happens? We get the cold shoulder from a bum like that! If it was the cold shoulder I was looking for, I could of gotten that in Newark! By gosh, sombody ought to punch the guy one in the snoz!"

"Oh Tom," said his wife, touching his arm, "he just

doesn't *know* any better! Didn't you see how he refused the money?"

"Well, he's not too old to learn, is he? He's a *nut,* if you ask me!"

Candy wanted to scoop the holy man up in her arms and run to the temple as fast as she could. Fortunately though, at that moment the tourists began turning away toward one of the picturesque side streets.

"We saw the Hindu rope-trick this morning," one of the women was saying, "a little boy climbed right up into the sky and out of sight—Goodness, I'll bet he hadn't had a bath in a month! Why they let their children get so dirty is beyond me!"

"There's a guy down this street supposed to have a 'flying-carpet,' " said a big-stomached man wearing a floral sport shirt and smoking a cigar, ". . . gives six rupees to the buck too—I don't like the black-market idea myself, but with these prices, who's gotta choice? Know what I mean?"

All this sort of talk just made Candy wring her hands in grief—she only hoped that the holy man hadn't heard and become upset. She wanted to kiss him, or in some way reassure him, but was uncertain whether she should and so merely walked along slowly behind him.

Although they were only about a block from the temple, the holy man's progress was so astonishingly slow that an hour passed before they reached the great steps—whereupon the holy man, like a snail coming to an impasse, merely turned away and began to inch along in another direction. He wasn't going to the temple after all! Good Grief! thought Candy, and at just that moment the temple clock sounded three and she remembered her appointment with the travel office—where she was to complete arrangements for her journey to Tibet—and she had to fly back down Zen Boulevard to the American Express.

A week later, Candy had gotten herself a little attic room in Lhasa, the holy center of Tibet. The American Express in Lhasa had been extremely helpful in finding her a place where the landlady would bring Candy a bowl of porridge each morning in exchange for the girl's assistance two hours a day in winding yak-yarn onto a spindle.

The house was only a short distance from the fabulous temple of Zen-Dowa, and Candy went there every day for meditation, sitting before the huge image of Buddha and focusing all her attention on the nose tip of the great idol.

When she arrived at the temple this afternoon, the sky above Lhasa was overcast deeply to the hue of rich slate, and Candy paused on the steps of the temple to look out at the snow-peaked mountains against this backdrop of foreboding; the white-top mountains appeared to her allegorically as the bright pinnacles of hope in a trouble-darkened world. She was extremely happy in her new life and did a little twirl of joy now on the great temple porch. The precious girl was still wearing the simple Cracker garment, which, as she twirled, billowed out to permit a glimpse of her darling dimpled knees and a marvelous and tantalizing bit above. It was then that she noticed, sitting in the corner, the holy man she had seen in Calcutta. How on earth had he gotten to Lhasa! Had he inched his way up the Himalayas? It looked as though he might have—he was enshelled in a crust of mud, dung and ash, his hair so matted that it was more like clay than anything else—and Candy was sure that he was in the coveted sixth stage of spiritual advancement; she herself was still always fresh and sweet . . . she had had six more of the simple Cracker shifts made and so she had a fresh change each day. She could not help staring in awe and reverence at this holy dung-man, who, as in Calcutta, seemed entirely unaware of her presence, either now or earlier when her twirl of joy had flashed a dazzling stretch of superb ivory thigh.

Then it suddenly began to rain. The holy man was sitting near the edge of the porch, only half sheltered, and drops of rain were falling on him. Despite her shyness, Candy couldn't bear the idea of his saintly dung-crust being damaged and she rushed over to him impulsively and began to pull him up and away toward the temple door. He was quite thin and pliable and made no resistance whatever, allowing himself to be taken inside the temple, and then seated beside the girl in front of the great image of the holy Buddha.

Candy began her meditation at once, concentrating all her attention on the single spot, the tip of Buddha's nose. It was wonderful for her—all her life it had always been *she* who had been needed by someone else—mostly boys— and now at last she had found someone that she herself needed . . . Buddha! And yet, because of her early orientation, of always being the needed one (except by Daddy!), there was something vaguely dissatisfying and incomplete about it. If only the Buddha needed her! But she knew of course that this was a silly feeling and would in time be overcome. She had already begun to think of the Buddha in a personal, almost human way. "My big friend," she sometimes said to herself. She glanced at the holy man sitting beside her. He seemed to be paying no attention to her or Buddha, but was simply gazing ahead, into infinity it seemed, while on the roof of the temple now the rain beat down terrifically and an occasional gigantic clap of thunder seemed to make the huge structure shudder to its foundations.

Candy returned her thought and concentration to the Buddha's nose, and put every last ounce of her little meditative power into it—and at that very instant a fantastic thing happened: an astounding crash of sound that seemed to split the earth itself and a tremendous flash of fire which filled the great vaulted roof of the temple while everything around seemed to sway and crumple as though the end of the world had surely come—for the great temple had been struck by lightning! Above them the huge Buddha loomed uncertainly for a breathtaking moment, then, in monumental slow motion, it toppled forward, pitching headlong to the temple floor in a veritable explosion.

Although it seemed to fall right on top of them, Candy and the holy man were miraculously unscathed, and were left bunched together, half buried in the rubble. In the tumult of the crash, Candy had been flung against the holy man frontally so that now they were pressed tightly together lengthwise. It was extremely awkward, for the young girl's shift had been forced well above her waist and her shapely bare limbs now were locked about the holy man's loins. She struggled to free herself but this only succeeded in agitating her precious and open honeypot against the holy man's secret parts—which were now awakening after so many years and slowly breaking through the rotten old loincloth that swaddled them! Good Gosh, thought Candy,

when she realized what was happening, and in fact, felt the
holy man's taut member ease an inch or two into her tight
little lamb-pit. She quickly turned her head to see behind
her and to determine what was pinioning them there. And
she saw that a part of the huge Buddha had just missed
them by inches, and was pressing firmly against her back;
it seemed to be balanced in a precarious way and in danger
of slipping—and, even as she thought this, she saw that it *was*
in fact slipping, forward, and against her; it was a section
of her beloved Buddha's face—the nose! And a truly incredible thing was happening—it was slipping into Candy's
marvelous derriere! "Good Grief!" said the girl, half
aloud, trying to move forward a little—which merely had
the effect of securely embedding the holy man's member
deeply into her ever-sweetening pudding-pie.

Above them the lightning bolt had opened a sizable hole
at the top of the roof and the summer rain was pouring in
on them now in torrents. It had wetted the tip of the
Buddha's nose, which did seem, thus lubricated, to be undeniable as it moved slowly into Candy's coyly arched
tooky—the warm wet nose of Buddha, the beloved spot of
her meditation! Not a wholly unpleasant sensation for the
adorable girl as it gracefully eased into her perfect bottom;
and it was then that she realized, with the same lightning
force of miracle which had split the roof, that wonder of
wonders, *the Buddha, too, needed her!* And so with a
sigh of indulgence she stopped her shy squirming and
gave herself up fully to her idol, one hand behind her,
stroking his cheek, as she gradually began the esoteric Exercise Number Four—and only realizing after a minute that
this movement was having a definite effect on the situation

in her honey-cloister as well, forcing the holy man's member deeply in and out as it did, and she turned to him at once, wanting to tell him that it *wasn't* meant the way it seemed certainly, but she was stricken stone dumb by what she saw—for the warm summer rain had worked its wonders there as well, washing the crust of dung and ash away completely, leaving the face clean, bright, and all too recognizable, as the eyes glittered terrifically while the hopeless ecstasy of his huge pent-up spasm began, and sweet Candy's melodious voice rang out through the temple in truly mixed feelings:

"GOOD GRIEF—IT'S DADDY!"